The Path of Swords

Martin Swinford

The Song of Amhar
Book One

Gable Press

email: gablepress@outlook.com

Contents

One – The Warrior

"You think you chose to be here, but you did not. You are here because hundreds of years ago a king decided you should be. You may think you are strong, that for you it will be easy, or you may think you have no chance and you are scared about what is to come. You may be angry that you have been forced here against your will, or you may be excited about being away from home. None of that matters. You are here to learn to fight and to kill. You will succeed or die in the attempt. Welcome second sons, welcome to the Guild of the Sword."

Luan lifted his eyes from the figure on the low stage at the centre of the hall. Faded flags hung from the vast roof-beams high above him and ancient coats of arms hung on the walls flanked by windows etched with heraldic symbols from long gone noble families. Across the arch high above were carved the words "Lest Ye Second Son Keep the Kingdom".

"How old is this place?" he thought. "How many have sat here listening to the speech of introduction?"

His gaze shifted down and he looked around the ranks of boys that surrounded him. There must have been about two hundred, although the room could have held many more.

Each of them had made the journey, leaving home on the last day of the summer of their fourteenth year. Such was the lot of a second son. Born to serve the kingdom, born to be a warrior, born to be a Klaideem.

His earliest memory was of his uncle, Marius, arriving one late summer evening. Luan must have been about five years old at the time but he would always recall the sound of horses' hooves on the path. He had waited so long for this moment. His uncle, the warrior, the great Klaideem himself was coming to see them. Luan stared eagerly into the dusk, his eyes straining to catch a first glimpse of this mysterious figure.

He was not to be disappointed. As the last of the light faded into darkness, Luan saw the silhouette of the knight appear where the path crested the brow of the hill above his father's hall. He heard the stamp of hoof and snort of breath as the horse made its careful way down towards them. Then at last he was there, a towering figure on horseback. Luan, suddenly shy, slipped behind his mother's skirts for safety. His older brother, Ban, stood as tall as an eight year old could next to their father.

"Hail Klaideem!" Their father spoke the words formally.
"Hail Cunbran and well met!" replied Marius, his words holding genuine warmth as he dismounted.
"Well met indeed!" Luan's father replied and a smile broke out on his face as he stepped forward and clasped his

brother in a firm embrace. Marius laughed and threw his arms around his brother, and then looked past him to the two small boys.
“And who are these fine warriors?” he asked, “Your new bodyguard?”
“My sons of course: I present to you Ban and Luan.”
“Hail Ban,” Marius said, smiling at the boy. Then he paused and knelt down.
“Hail second son,” he said to the five year old Luan.

That was the day that Luan started to realise that his destiny was different from his older brother's. That in time Ban would be the Cunbran, the Clan-Chief, and that it was Luan, the second son, who might one day become one of the Klaideem, the sword warriors.

Two – Luan's Choice

"The first test on the path of swords is the one you have already passed. The day you left your home and family was the day you started that first test and the day you arrived here it was complete. Those that failed that test are the ones that did not make it here, the ones who have met with death on the road, or strayed from the path, or decided to follow another."

Luan looked again at the empty seats in the hall. He tried to imagine the boys who could have been sitting there but for chance or misfortune. Had he known the dangers of the journey, would he have had the courage to set out?

All through the summer Luan had felt as if a hard lump was congealing in his stomach. He had long known what was expected of him, that the choice that faced him was really no choice at all. What else could he have done? Refused the calling? Choose to stand in the shadows and do nothing but watch his brother become Clan Chief? Shame would follow him all his days, he would be an embarrassment to his family.

He thought often of his uncle Marius, and of the last time he saw him. The warrior had been a hero to Luan throughout the boy's life. Ever since that first meeting Luan had looked upon Marius as something out of one of the old legends. The knight in armour who would appear suddenly, riding out of the darkness and just as quickly be gone. Often he would bring some small present for Ban and Luan and one well remembered time he had brought toy armour and weapons, a helmet and spear for Ban and a sword and shield for Luan. That summer they had refought all the old battles of history, the paddocks had been their battlefields and the haystacks their castles to be captured and defended.

But the last time had been different. Luan had been ten years old and Marius arrived without the ready humour of his previous visits. He had said only a brief word to Luan and Ban, ruffling their hair as he walked in and closeted himself with their father. The boys waited. They could just make out the low voices of their father and uncle. After a while their mother brought food and drink and boys caught a fragment of conversation, broken off. "...invasion?" their father's voice and "...testing us" in reply.
"There's going to be a battle." Ban's voice, wavering between child and adult, betrayed excitement. A sudden sense of fear swept through Luan and tears started in his eyes. He blinked them back, struggling to control his feelings. Foreboding filled him with a new awareness of the possibility of loss.
"Chores to do you two!" Their mother seemed to have a serious aversion to Luan and Ban doing nothing. "Ban! That woodpile's getting low, get the axe. Luan! Fetch some water and then you can finish weeding my garden."

Pulling the weeds from around the vegetables kept Luan busy but his mind was still in turmoil. As he worked his way along the rows he listened for the sound of his uncle and his father leaving the room where they were closeted. Finally he heard the bang of the door and the sound of voices. He dropped the trowel and sprinted round to the front of the hall just in time to hear his father order a servant to saddle his uncle's horse. Luan skidded to a stop and then stood still, unsure now what to say but needing to somehow express his feelings. In the end he blurted out the simple distillation of a child's fears.
"Don't go!"
Marius looked at Luan and then walked towards him. He reached out and put his hand on Luan’s shoulder.
"I chose this path a long time ago Luan," he said. "I chose duty and honour that day, and I cannot turn aside now."
Marius took a step back and drew the long sword from over his shoulder. He placed it point down between them, knelt and beckoned Luan forward.
"Come here."
Luan stepped forward, aware that something important was happening. Marius reached out and took Luan’s hands in his own. He placed one on the hilt of the sword and the other on the crosspiece.
"This is how I took the oath to follow the path of swords, wherever it would lead me. One day you will kneel as I did and make your choice. I know that you will bring our family honour."

Luan never saw Marius again. Four weeks later a trader brought news of a huge battle to the south. The Imperial Legions halted and pushed back. A victory but at huge cost, and a name, Banduan. Three weeks after that, Marius' sword was delivered to the hall.

It was cool the morning that Luan began his journey. They stood at the top of the hill, the sky just starting to shade to blue above them. To the east the horizon was tinged with red as behind the wisps of cloud the sun began its ascent. Luan looked down at his mother standing in front of the hall, Ban, tall and close to manhood, by her side, wreaths of mist about their feet. He looked back to his father standing in front of him, holding the sword that was all that he had left of his brother.

"Luan, you need to know that I will always be proud of you. No matter what choice you make, you will always be my son."

Luan returned his gaze. Now he was at the point of choosing, his doubts had fled.

"Thank you father, but I have made my choice. I will follow my uncle."

"And he will be proud of you, as he watches from the lands of the dead." With a swift motion he drew the sword and plunged the tip into the ground between them.

“The time has come!” he said.

Luan knelt and grasped the hilt and crosspiece just as his uncle had showed him three years earlier. His father placed

his hand on Luan’s head and spoke formally.
"Luan ap Garioch, second son of the house of Artran, this is the day of choosing. How do you choose?"
"I choose the path of swords," intoned Luan
"Do you then give up your claim to the lands of your birth?"
"I do."
"Do you swear to be honourable and just, to follow the path without delay and never stepping aside?”
"I do so swear."
"Then stand second son and receive your birthright."
Luan stood and as he did his father lifted the sword high, then sheathed it and held it out, balanced on the palms of both hands. Luan took the sword. It felt heavy but somehow right. Almost he could feel the presence of Marius beside him.
"Go well my son."
Luan met his father eyes. He had no words left. He slung the sword over his shoulder, turned and set off down the hill.

It was later that day that he saw the walkers for the first time.

He wasn't sure what he noticed first. Was it the dust of their feet? Or was it the low hum that seemed to accompany them as they travelled the rough track that dropped down out the hills to meet the path he had chosen. Reaching the crossroads first, he stopped and waited; now recognising the low hum as some kind of chant, the words indistinguishable.

When they reached him they stopped and fell silent. There were nine of them; each dressed in long grey cloaks, their faces and heads covered in hoods through which only their eyes were visible. Their gaze was penetrating and Luan suddenly felt afraid.

"Where do you walk to?" he asked.
The leader of the group stared at him. Close to, Luan could see that stitched to the fabric of his grey cloak was a seemingly random collection of metal objects: coins, buckles, bits of harness, and old nails among things unidentifiable.
A few seconds passed, then the leader broke his silence.
"Where do we walk?" he called.
"We walk the paths!" The answer, spoken in unison by the group had the feeling of ritual.
"How long shall we walk?" intoned the leader.
"Until the land is free!"
The leader turned his gaze to Luan.
"We walk the paths," he said. "Do you follow?"
Luan was filled with a desire to go with them. Fleeting visions of strange lands filled his eyes. For a moment the answer "I will follow!" took form in his mouth but then the weight of the sword on his back dragged him back to reality. He stared at the strange figure before him.
"I take the path of swords," he replied, the words coming

unbidden.
The leader looked him in the eye, his gaze unwavering.
“Follow or stand aside.”
Luan stepped to one side. The strange, low chanting started again as the walkers set off. He stood and watched as they vanished into the distance, never once looking back.

Three – The Farm

"You are now part of the story of this land. Your part is all the more vital because there are now so few of us."

Luan had been walking for three days when he saw the smoke in the distance. He had avoided people so far but now, cold and hungry, he decided that he needed to seek shelter. Taking a path that seemed to lead in the right direction he crossed the stretch of wind swept heath and started heading downhill. Suddenly a tight valley opened up in front of him and there, nestled snugly in the bottom, was a small farmstead. The smoke was coming from a hall surrounded by smaller buildings, grain stores and sheep pens mostly. The path made its way around the side of valley heading downwards until had almost come full circle and Luan carefully made his way down, slipping occasionally on the loose stones that rain had left behind. Luan had just reached the valley floor when a dog started barking, a deep, gruff, complaining sound. A short stocky man stepped into view in the open area in front of the hall. He was roughly dressed with short wiry hair and grizzled beard shot through with grey and white. His eyes looked keenly at the stranger before him, taking in Luan's appearance, his stance, his clothes and the sword on his back. Finally he spoke.
"That's a fine lookin' sword yer got there young sir." His

accent was thick and strange, hammering home to Luan how little he knew of this world he was now adrift in.
“It was my uncle's.” The words sounded pathetic to Luan but the man smiled.
“Well,” he said. “You're not the first, and you sure won't be the last. Come on.”

He turned and led the way across the yard to the doorway of the hall. A piece of sacking was nailed to the lintel for a makeshift screen, hanging about two thirds of the way down the opening. A wisp of smoke curled out of the door as the man pushed the sacking aside and ducked through the low doorway. Luan followed.
Inside it was dark, the air thick with smoke. A small group of people were sitting round a fire in the centre of the room while in the shadows children chased and wrestled, oblivious to the presence of a stranger.
“Look to, Anna, we have a guest!”
One of the villagers stood up and as Luan’s eyes adjusted to the gloom he made out the homely features of a woman of about middle age.
“What have you found now Gareth?” She asked.
“Tis a young lad following the sword, my love.” replied the farmer.
Luan had thought Gareth was a labourer but now he revised his opinion. His host was obviously the chief of this small settlement. Looking around the hall Luan realised that there were some signs of comfort if not wealth. The sleeping platforms around the sides were hung with drapes and the

some of the beds had embroidered quilts. Rag rugs made the floors of those platforms more comfortable and the straw on the floor of the main hall was clean. One of the figures near the fire stood up and started busying herself with the pots and cauldrons that were arranged carefully to make the most of the available heat. The figure was slight beneath a hooded robe and when she cast a quick glance at Luan he caught a glimpse of blonde hair and pale blue eyes.
"My eldest daughter Lyssia." There was a slight note of warning in Gareth's voice. Then he smiled.
"And these others are my wife, Anna, and her parents Brenna and Mack."
The old couple looked up. The woman smiled. Her face was lined and her hair grey, but her bright eyes were welcoming.
"Hello lad," she said.
The man, Mack, looked up briefly, nodded and then returned his concentration to the object on his lap. It looked like some kind of musical instrument with strings and a fretboard, but it was nothing like the lute that Luan remembered his mother playing.
"Aha!" Exclaimed Mack "Got it!" He pulled out one of the strings and started to wind it around his fingers.
"Please forgive my old dad," said Anna. "He gets so into his harp playing he forgets his manners sometimes. Here, come where it's warm. I expect you're half-starved as well. What are we calling you then?"
"Er, it's Luan, and thanks." He sat down near the fire.
"What kind of instrument is that?"

Mack looked up, a spark in his eye as he realised that he had the one thing that musicians and old men crave, an audience.
"Ah! Like music do yer?"
"Yes, I mean, my mother used to play the lute."
"A fine instrument." The old man made the announcement with some authority "You don't play though!"
"How can you tell?" asked Luan, surprised.
In reply Mack reached out and turned Luan's hands over and lifted them to display the fingertips.

"Too soft, not like mine!" he said and held up his hand so that Luan could see the hard callouses on the end of each finger. Luan looked more closely at his new companion, revising his first impression of a harmless old man. Mack certainly looked old, his skin was weathered and what remained of his hair was a wispy white tonsure around an uneven brown scalp. In the centre of his forehead was an old scar and his beard was patchy and grey. His eyes though were alive, he had a ready smile and emotions seemed to flit across his face like sunlight and shadows across a hillside on a windy day. He lifted up the instrument so that Luan could see it more easily.
"Now young man," he started. "What we have 'ere is very special..."
"Oh let the lad be, dad!" Anna interrupted. "He's tired and he don't want you goin' on at 'im. Here Luan." She handed Luan a bowl. "There's some stew. Never mind my old dad, he just likes someone to talk at."

"I don't mind." Luan protested.
"Now don't you encourage 'im." Anna's mother, Brenna, joined in. "Old fool'll talk the hind leg off of a goat if you give him a chance."
A black look clouded Mack's face. "Goats pay me more attention than you do anyway!"
"That's as because you smell like 'em!" replied his wife with a cackle.
"That does it!" Mack exploded to his feet "I'm wasting no more time on those that don't appreciate me."
Mack attempted to storm out but was hindered by the fact that he was in his stocking feet. To the delight of his family he was reduced to scrabbling in the straw for his boots and then trying to make a dignified exit while hopping as he tried to put them on, all the while muttering to himself. Luan caught a snatch of his tirade.
"Played at the courts of Kings and Princes and reduced to this."
As he ducked under the sacking in the doorway, Brenna gestured for quiet.
"Listen." she said.
From outside came Mack's voice, clear and strong.

"Ladies and gentleman of the audience! I present to you, that noblest of Troubadours, Mack!"
The answer was a chorus of bleating.
"He does make me laugh!" Giggled Brenna.

It was warm by the fire and Luan soon found it difficult to keep his eyes open. Brenna tapped her daughter's arm.

"The poor lad's half asleep Anna."
"Aye, he is that. Gareth!" She called out. "Take the lad and find him a sleeping spot."
Luan allowed himself to be led toward the side of the hall where Gareth showed him a rough bed, a rug and a blanket over a layer of straw. Muttering his thanks Luan lay down, slipping quickly into a deep sleep.

He woke suddenly. Images of the sea and sky filled his head and music that he thought he dreamt remained as he opened his eyes. He could tell that time had passed; it was dark and only the fire lit the hall. Luan could see Mack's silhouette, the comical old man transformed into a nobler figure by the act of playing. The music maintained the dream like state. Mack's fingers creating a tapestry of haunting sound as they danced over the strings. Then the girl, Lyssia, pushed back the hood of her robe and sang. Luan was transfixed. Her voice had a purity that seemed almost otherworldly. She sang with her eyes closed, lost in some other state and as she sang the words caught Luan and transported him back to the strange seas of his dream and he slept again.

Five great ships from out of the night,
Riding the waves to the land of light.
Amhar the strong, with foresight blessed,
Follows his destiny into the west.

Four – A Companion

"You faced many dangers on your journey, you will face many more. Some threats are obvious. The spear, the sword, the arrow, these you expect and so you guard against them. Beware those threats that are less obvious for they can be your downfall."

Luan woke late the next morning. He lay for a second or two, first getting his bearings and then luxuriating in a real bed, simple perhaps but better by far than the ground he had slept on for the previous two nights. Then he sat up, threw off the coverings and looked round for his boots. He was alone, which did not surprise him. He was used to the farming way of life and knew that the daily work started early. Luan may have been the son of the chief but that had not shielded him from hard work.

Luan stepped outside into a bright, crisp morning. The familiar sounds of farm life surrounded him. He could hear the cows grunting and blowing as Gareth herded them back up onto the hillside pasture after their morning milking. In one of the sheds he could hear bleating as the goats took their turn in giving up their precious milk. He wondered who was milking and his thoughts turned to Lyssia. He had thought little about her when he first arrived being more concerned with food and warmth, but her clear voice had followed him into his dreams, and he wished now he had

paid her more attention. He tried to picture her face and then suddenly she was there before him as if he had somehow summoned the girl with his thoughts. The pail of milk in her hand brought him back to reality and he realised he was just standing, staring and not talking.
"Hello," he said finally.
Lyssia smiled at him and he realised that she was beautiful. He had noticed her blue eyes and blonde hair the night before but now he saw she had high cheekbones and about her face was a perfect symmetry.
"Would you like something to eat?"
Luan realised that he was still staring like a fool.
"Er, yes, thank you, if you're not busy?" Of course she was busy. A strange paralysis had struck his lips and as a result he was drowning in a conversation.
"It's no trouble," she said gently and then ducked into the hall. Luan took a deep breath as if he had momentarily surfaced and was about to follow her inside, when Mack walked round the corner of the building.
"Take care lad!" he said, to Luan's surprise.
"What do you mean?"
"Does Gareth seem to you as the carefree type who leaves his beautiful daughter in the care of a complete stranger?"
Luan thought back to the night before and remembered the note of warning when Gareth had introduced his daughter.
"Well no, but..."
"Come on boy, think! Where's her Ma? Where's old Brinna as would usually be watchin' 'er?"
"You don't mean?"

"Now you're startin' to think!"
A cold feeling came over Luan as he suddenly realised what was happening.
"But why? I mean, I'm the second son. I've given it all up."
Mack, his hand to forehead, let out a sigh.
"So young to be let loose in the world! Look, 'ere's how it works. Gareth, 'e don't own this land. He holds it for the Cunbran, the clan chief like your Da, and 'e's happy as 'e is, doing what 'is family 'as done for longer n they can recall. But Anna, she's got ideas. An maybe you don't have any land but..."
"I can own it in the future."
"Now we're getting there! Lyssia an' you gets wed. Your Da pays a dowry. You buy the land. And Anna, she's no longer a farmer's wife, she is landowner. Through her lass maybe but that don't matter to her."
"But surely they don't think I would give up the sword path so easily!"
"If you were found alone in there with her it wouldn't matter would it?"
At last Luan could see the snare that had been laid for him. By the customs of the Kingdom, should a boy and a girl of marriageable age spend a night under the same roof without a chaperone they were considered to be married. If he were discovered alone with Lyssia in the hall in the early morning it would be easy for her parents to claim that her virtue was ruined, and his only honourable action would have been to agree to marry her. A horrible thought struck him.

"What about last night?"
Mack smiled "You know I had just finished entertaining the goats when I saw Gareth and Anna slip away to the barn. Then a bit after that Brinna came out and went over to the hayloft where she made herself right comfortable."
Luan felt the life drain out of him.
"Then it's too late, what am I going to do?"
"Aah, don't worry lad. Thing is I thought to myself, well, with them out the way there's a nice spot close to the fire going free. So I slipped right in."
"So you were there?" Luan hardly dared to think it.
"All night. Slept sound and warm too!"
Relief washed over Luan.
"Thank you, I mean, how can I pay you back?"
Mack's grin put Luan in mind of a cat who is owed a favour by a mouse.
"Don't worry lad! I will tell you exactly how you're goin' to pay me back, but it can wait while breakfast."
Mack turned and stepped inside. Luan, feeling slightly less relieved, followed him.

It might have been his imagination but it seemed to Luan that Lyssia wasn't overjoyed to see Mack. She still smiled when she brought them some bread and cheese and a cup of milk but then busied herself with chores rather than talk to them. Mack chuckled to himself and then winked at Luan. Luan ate quickly and then got ready to leave, putting his arm through the strap of the great sword so that it hung across his back and slinging his pack from his shoulder. He

said goodbye to the girl, expressed sorrow that her parents were busy and asked that she pass on his thanks. Lyssia looked at him helplessly and for a brief moment Luan felt a pang of regret.
"Come on then lad" Mack was dressed for walking, with a stout stick in his hand and a pack on his back.
"Where do you think you're going?" The voice in the doorway rang with suspicion. Anna stood there, the kindly woman of the previous night replaced by a more formidable character altogether. Mack stayed calm.
"Well I've been thinking for a while I should do something more to help out and as you are always pointing out how little use I am in the way of farming I thought as though I'd step over to Crosland. Make a bit of money playing in the tavern. And as the boy is on his way I thought I'd walk with him. Two is safer than one int it?"
Anna looked suspicious. "Make a bit of money? Spend it all on ale more like!" She sniffed and then snorted a kind of 'huh' under breath, clearly unhappy but unable to do anything about it.
"Oh get off with yer then you old fool!"
Mack bowed deeply and then strode out with an ironic swagger. Luan hurried after him, trying to be as polite as is possible in such a situation.
"Thank you, you've been very kind..."
"Yes, well..." Anna's desire to save face stopped her from making any pointed comment and with a struggle she reverted to the role of the friendly farmer's wife. "You're welcome young sir. Good luck on your journey," she said

but couldn't resist one last parting shot. "Just don't let Mack lead you astray!"
Unsure how to respond, Luan smiled and nodded and then ran to catch up with the old man who had already started up the path.

Five – The World of the Spirit

"No doubt you have travelled with strange companions on your way, and no doubt you will do so again. Part of the first test is learning who you can trust. Friendship often comes unlooked for, and assistance found in unlikely places."

Luan followed Mack up the slope out the valley. Despite his age the tall, slightly gaunt figure seemed unaffected by a climb that left Luan feeling decidedly winded by the time they reached the top.
"Come on lad!" encouraged Mac. "We've a fair way to go and I'd like to put some distance between us and the farm before we stop."
Mack set off across the open heath and Luan followed along the sheep track behind him. It was a bright day and curlews and plovers wheeled in the blue sky. Purple heather stretched away to either side of them interspersed with patches of tall cotton grass that danced in the breeze. A pheasant shot up as they passed startling Luan with its "cuchuck cuchuck cuchuck" sound as it flew low over their heads.
"Just missed your dinner lad!" laughed Mack.
As a growing boy, food was never far from Luan's thoughts.
"Are we going to eat when we get to Crosland?" he asked.
"Not going there!" replied Mack over his shoulder.

"What? But you said to Anna!"
"Well, I had to say something didn't I?" Mack looked slightly sheepish. "Couldn't say I was leaving could I?"
Luan was astonished
"You're running away!" he accused.
"No! Not running, more sort of, moving on." Mack stopped, turned and gave Luan a long look. "You're going to be shocked, I can tell." Mack sighed "Look, I'll explain. Sit down."
They sat on the long yellow grass at the side of the path as Mack told his story.

"I've always been a traveller. As long as I can remember I've been out on the road. Done many things in my time, seen stuff you wouldn't believe!"
"You were a minstrel."
"Aye, I was. More'n that at times, but minstrel was my first and best calling. Travelled all over. Played and sang in places you ain't even heard of."
Luan thought to himself that he hadn't heard of many places but he didn't interrupt.
"Anyway, thing is, you get tired after a while. And I was on the road for close on fifty years! Weary I was and I had a notion that I needed to go home, settle down. So I headed back to the only family I had. That farmstead was my cousins but when I finally made it back, he'd passed on. His son, Gareth, ran the farm with his wife, Anna and her mother."
"Brinna!" Exclaimed Luan.

"Exactly," replied Mack. "And Brinna, well, she took a shine to me straight off. Anna never approved, thought me a vagabond. But Brinna, she knew what she wanted. And so we settled down together, like Man and Wife, although we never made it official. Anna used to call me Da just so as it would seem respectable." Mack paused and looked back across the moors to the crease in the ground that hinted of the valley beyond. He sighed, and when he continued his voice was soft.
"And I really meant to make a go of it. It was fine at first. I was warm and fed, and Brinna couldn't do enough for me. But after a while I started to feel tied down, the road's in my blood, you see? And Brinna knew I reckon, and she started nagging at me, and she didn't want to listen to my songs anymore, just laughed and called me an old fool. And seeing you, young and going out into the world adventuring, well it stirred it all up again. And when I saw what they was about I thought here's my chance and I couldn't let them trap you too."
He looked at Luan and said in a slightly defensive tone.
"I never wanted to upset her!"
Luan didn't know what to say. The conversation was like no other he had experienced. He had expected his journey to be dangerous and strange, but sitting on a hill while an old man made excuses about running away from his wife seemed crazy.
Not knowing what to say, Luan just sat and looked at the view. It was warm on the hillside in the morning sun, the kind of warmth that you take for granted during the

summer but you savour in autumn, knowing that you're going to have carry its memory through the long winter months. Luan suddenly realised he was happy. A question occurred to him.
"So where are we going then?"
Mack looked up and then suddenly snapped out of his gloom.
"How about up this hill for a start!"
He jumped to his feet and held out his hand to pull Luan up.
"Come on lad!"

The path followed a gradual rise in the land. Up ahead Luan could see a low mound rising against the sky. While the surrounding land was rough scrub and bracken, the hill was covered in an even coat of green grass. It seemed unworldly and he said as much to Mack.
"Unworldly! Well there's those that would agree with you."
"What do you mean?" Luan was curious.
"Well it's one of the old places, a burial mound most likely." Mack pointed and then with his finger traced the symmetry of the hill against the skyline. "A chieftain, or a great warrior, placed up here between the earth and the sky, guarding the lands of the tribe forever."
For a brief moment Luan could almost see it. A double line of the tribe holding torches in the twilight as a group of warriors bore their chieftain on their shoulders, slowly pacing up the path to a low door in the freshly raised hill.

"But why unworldly?"
"You mean you don't know?" Mack looked surprised. "About the doors between the realms? About the spirit world and those that live there?"
"No, I mean I know that there are stories, old wives tales that simple folk tell..." Luan stopped and looked at Mack.
"Aah! Simple folk like me you mean?" Mack's voice was gruff but the smile in his eyes told a different story.
"No! Not at all, it's just..." Luan paused and looked at Mack unsure as to how much of his life to share with his new companion. "Well my Mother,..."
"Let me guess, she says you should only believe in what you can see and touch."
"Er, yes. And smell and hear and taste. She says everything else is just superstition."
Mack nodded.
"And your Ma never held with any of the festivals I'm guessing."
"No." Luan had never really questioned it before. His mum had been so sure and it all seemed so sensible. Yet standing here on the hillside with the mound above him, Luan felt as if he was on the threshold of another world.
"Your mum sounds like one of the Creidheich." said Mack.
"What are they?"
"Sceptics, they don't believe in gods, or spirits or other worlds, pretty harmless but very boring."
Mack started back up the path. Luan felt slightly offended but he had to admit, if only to himself, that when he was younger he had been intensely jealous of the families that

celebrated the feasts and festivals that marked the turning of the seasons. He hurried up the path after Mack, curiously turning ideas over in his mind.
"What do you believe?" He called after Mack.
"That's a very personal question to ask someone you've only just met!" He replied over his shoulder.
They stopped where the path met the short green grass that marked the beginning of the strange mound. Here the path bent round to the right dropping a short way then rising steeply rather than carrying on across the mound. Mack turned to Luan.
"I don't know about believing as such, but I tell you what, I would think twice before stepping off this side of the path."
"But it's just grass!"
"Yeah? You do it then!"
Luan hesitated. At home he had been happy to follow his mother's lead. Stories of spirits and ghosts were just that, stories for children and left behind when you grew up. But something warned him there was danger here. Senses that he had never known he had were screaming at him but at the same time something drew him on. He felt Mack staring as if this was a test and in a moment of bravado he stepped off the path.
As soon as his feet touched the grass he felt a jolt of energy course up his legs and knew he had made a stupid mistake. The light dimmed suddenly and the ground seemed to slip away. With a feeling of terror he felt his legs giving way as if his bones were no longer rigid and he stumbled. Then he felt Mack's hand grasp his arm. Immediately the ground

steadied, the sunlight returned and his legs were his own again. He stepped back onto the path.
"You alright there lad?" Mack was looking keenly at Luan, his expression almost fearful.
"Just stumbled that's all," replied Luan. His disorientation had disappeared so rapidly he almost believed he had just tripped or slipped, the rest of it just over-imagination brought on by Mack's words. He certainly didn't feel like discussing it, the whole experience had been so unnerving. He felt scared and confused, and needed time to think. He followed Mack round the edge of the burial mound and up to the ridge, being careful to stay on the path.

They were standing catching their breath after the steep climb when Luan asked Mack what he had meant about the different worlds. Mack turned and pointed to the path they had followed.
"See how the path bends to the right and comes up this side of the mound."
"Yes"
"Well the old stories have it that these mounds are doorways between the realms." Mack explained. "Not the only ones, but powerful places. Edges of things you see, shorelines are another one, where the sea meets the land..."
"And here the land meets the sky!" Replied Luan.
"Exactly! And times are the same. When it is neither night nor day then the barriers between this world and the spirit world are weaker. They say that if you come here at dawn or twilight you can hear the creatures of the spirit world!"

"So you never cross a burial mound?" Luan's practical view of the world was starting to assert itself. Mack heard the scepticism in Luan's voice.
"It's what some people believe. My thinking is, why take a risk?"
"What risk?"
"The old stories tell of people disappearing never to return, or turning up many years later not having aged at all."
This was too much for Luan, he had always dismissed such things as fairy stories and yet a little part of him was saying 'So what happened when you stepped off the path then?'
"Surely there is only this world?" he asked.
Mack looked at Luan.
"One world? Aye, maybe. But there are different realms. We experience the realm of life, which is what we see and taste and touch, but the realm of the spirit flows through it and over it."
Luan thought for a bit. "How do we know it's there if we can't see it?"
Mack pointed out over the hillside. "Can you see the grass moving?"
"Yes. It's being blown by the wind."
"Can you see the wind?"
Luan thought a bit more. "So we know the spirit world exists because we can see its effects?"
"See them, hear them, feel them." said Mack
"And is that where the gods come from? The spirit realm?"
Mack pulled a face and then pointed across the valley to a small village on the other side.

"See that windmill? Built by man to catch the power of the wind. Gods are pretty much the same!" And he set off down the hill. Luan, feeling more confused than ever, followed.

Six – A Rescue

"The Kingdom has faced enemies since the day it came into being. There are the enemies outside and inside our borders. Some plan to invade and conquer, wanting to add the rich lands of the Kingdom to their empires. Others raid into our lands in search of plunder, whether that is cattle, horses, gold or even slaves. Our duty is to be the guardians of the Kingdom, to keep an unceasing watch over its lands and people."

Mack and Luan made their way down the hillside following the sheep tracks that wound their way through the heather. Looking down, Luan could see the line of trees that marked the path of the river along the valley below them. The going got steeper and the heather gradually gave way to rough grass and gorse bushes. Very soon Mack was struggling with the slope, slipping and sliding where rain had reduced the path to patches of gravel.
"Are you all right?" the concern showed in Luan's voice.
"Not as young as I used to be lad!" Mack's smile suddenly disappeared as he slipped further down the hill, crying out in alarm. Luan scurried down after him, half skipping and half sliding on his backside as he desperately tried to catch up with Mack. At last he managed to grab the scruff of the old man's tunic and the pair of them finally came to halt, squashed up against the trunk of young birch that grew up out of the hillside. Mack groaned and then drew in his

breath with a sharp hiss as he tried to move.
"Are you hurt?" asked Luan.
"Just scrapes and bruises I reckon," replied Mack. "Ow!" he added as he tried to sit up.
Luan helped the old man into a more comfortable position and Mack let out a sign of relief as he leaned back against the tree.
"We'll just sit here for few minutes, catch our breath like," he said, and Luan took the opportunity to stretch out on the grass. His legs were trembling after the steep descent and he lay still, looking up at the sky and waited for them to recover. Watching the clouds above him he found himself imagining ships slipping quietly through the mist and he remembered the words of the song that Lyssia had sung the night before and he sang them quietly.

"Five great ships from out of the night
Riding the waves to the land of light"

"Mack?" he said "Where do those lines come from?"
"Hmm?" Mack had started to dose off.
"Hey! Mack!" Mack's eyes flicked open.
"What is it lad?" his voice querulous.
Luan repeated his question and Mack regarded him thoughtfully.
"It is a good tale and a long one that," he said. "It tells of Amhar the Strong and his journey into the land of the Shibaan. You know who Amhar was don't you lad?"
"Yes," replied Luan. "He was the first King."

"That's right," said Mack "And if you think about it you will see why he was called the strong. Imagine, he was just the leader of a small tribe on the west coast and he built the Kingdom. The land had never had just one ruler. For hundreds of years things had been the same, tribe fighting against tribe, with no one ever keeping the upper hand for long."
"So what was different about Amhar then?" Luan was starting to get interested.
"According to legend Amhar was no ordinary man. The tales tell that his mother was a seeress, she had the sight!"
"The sight?"
"She could see the future."
"That's not possible!" Luan's upbringing was starting to make itself felt again. Mack gave him a long look.
"Do you want to hear the story?"
"Yes!" Luan said. "Sorry."
Mack gave him a quick smile and then leant back, composed himself and began to speak, his voice taking on a quality that Luan had not heard before.

On the eve of the longest day of the year
When the moon shone red in the evening light
The spearman stood on the threshold strong
And guarded the clan home into the night
While the bats took wing and the dog fox barked
And the owl flew low over farm and field
In the hour before dawn in the dark of the night
A son to The Lord of the clan was born

But the banshee wailed in the place of the clan
As the moonlit boy was born
Three times the mother cried to the night
The sorrowful words of the second sight
"Born to be king over all the land,
Only in the west will you destiny find,
Born into sorrow, in hope to be raised
In time to be king, in old age betrayed"

Mack paused.
"So begins the tale of Amhar the Strong. Born under a full moon on the midsummer's eve and so blessed by moon magic and the sun god both, his mother dying in childbirth but only after foretelling his future as King. At least so the tales tell. It was over five hundred years ago." At that moment Mack looked almost as if he was feeling the full weight of those years himself, it seemed to Luan as if the old man's gaze was fixed not on the hills around them but on the distant past.
"Five Hundred Years!" echoed Luan. He could barely comprehend so long a time. "But what about the bit with the ships and the mist? That sounded like a good bit!"
"A good bit!" replied Mack in mock outrage. "One of the greatest of all the old tales, passed down through generations, the living history of our land, and you only want to hear 'a good bit'?"
Luan smiled. "Yes please."
"All right then," Mack grinned and leaned back again. "The 'good bit' you want starts after Amhar had won his first

battles and..."

Suddenly he was interrupted. Below them in the valley they could hear the sound of someone approaching. It sounded like someone was pushing their way through the brush by the side of the stream that flowed along the valley floor. Mack gestured to Luan who rolled over, wormed his way to the edge of the bluff and looked down. About twenty feet below him the stream ran clear over gravel and along its banks trees and bushes crouched low. On the far side of the stream was a well-worn track and the ground between was a mixture of boggy grass and gorse bushes. Luan could see that someone was following the bank of the stream and he thought it strange that they should ignore the obviously much easier path. Then he heard shouts and the sound of horses' hooves and realised why. Below him a figure broke free of the bushes and looked around wildly. Luan was surprised to see a boy, younger and slighter than himself, dirty and ragged from his flight. The boy looked as if he did not know where to turn, but then dashed across the stream and desperately threw himself at the steep slope immediately below Luan. The noise of pursuit was getting louder, Luan guessed several horses and riders. The curve in the valley bid them from sight but he judged the boy had a minute at most. Luan looked straight down the slope, the boy had made good progress at first but now he was struggling and Luan judged that he would never make it. Without stopping to think Luan locked his feet round the birch trunk and leaned out over the edge as far as he could. He stretched out his hand and shouted to the now clearly

frightened boy below.
"Here! Quickly!"
The boy looked up and Luan caught a glimpse of pale skin and dark eyes. Then in a last desperate effort the boy launched himself up the slope, grabbed Luan's hand and together they managed to scramble to safety.

The danger was not yet past. Mack pushed his hand out, palm downwards, signalling they should stay down as the noise of riders grew ever closer. From his position behind the tree he had a clear view as the group of horsemen swept round the corner and thundered by. Mack's sharp intake of breath hissed between his teeth.
"Slavers!"

The word cast a chill over Luan. To him there was only one association with that word, and that was the Pireacht. The name was a dark shadow throughout his childhood and probably that of every other child of the Kingdom. It conjured up images of faceless legions marching under the banners of a dark god from their lands far to the South, and the light of freedom snuffed out. In fact Luan knew very little about the reality of the Pireacht other than his uncle had died fighting them. That was enough.

"Have they gone?" The newcomer's voice was shaky.
"I think so, for now at least," answered Mack.
"Will they come back?" Luan did not want to sound afraid but he suddenly felt a long way from home. He stood so

that he could get a better view.
"I don't know." Mack was trying to look down the track
"Even these days they will want to travel quickly to avoid being caught. I suppose it depends how much the escapee is worth" and he turned his gaze onto the slight figure still panting on the hillside.
"Is a boy very valuable?" asked Luan.
"A boy?" Outrage had replaced the shakiness.
Mack looked at Luan and laughed. "Don't worry my dear, he's only just left home and he has a lot to learn!" And he held out his hand to the girl and helped her to her feet.
"You can call me Mack, and your unobservant saviour here is Luan."
Luan suddenly blushed deep red.

Her name was Bridie and she was a couple of inches shorter than Luan and he guessed maybe a year younger. Her sandy hair was short and roughly cut. She wore a loose tunic and leggings and her feet were bare. Her face and hands were scratched and cut from her escape and her large brown eyes were intense as she studied Luan with the same interest that he did her. Their eyes met for a moment, and then Luan dropped his gaze and started to turn away. A small hand on his arm stopped him and he turned back.
Bridie smiled.
"Thank you."
Luan was tongue tied.
"It's er, it's, er ok," he said at last
Mack was grinning broadly. Luan gave him a look.

"Hadn't we better get out of here?"
Mack's expression grew serious and he nodded.
"I think they're gone but we should be on our way. The question is: which is our way?"
Luan looked around. The slavers had headed along the valley which ran roughly north-south. In the opposite direction, to the south, was the small village that he and Mack had seen from the top of the hill. To the east, on the other side of the track, the land rose again to another ridge.
"East," he said. "Once we're over that ridge we'll be very hard to find."
Mack looked sceptical. "Yes, but while we're heading up we'll be visible for miles."
"At least we won't get caught on the track. We'd have no chance then!"
Bridie looked at the mismatched pair that were her new companions. Even though she had only known them a few minutes she decided to stick with them. It was unusual for her to be so quick to trust someone but there was something about the pair of them that inspired confidence and Luan had saved her without any thought for himself. He clearly didn't think anything of it either, which she found puzzling. Most of the boys she had known would have expected to be praised as a hero but Luan seemed embarrassed if anything. She found him interesting to look at. Bridie could tell that he was going to be tall and reasonably well built but probably on the slim side. He had a firm mouth and the set of his jaw showed character, he was yet to show any sign of down on his face. His hair was dark with a fringe that he

was always pushing away from his eyes and his face was honest but with a sense that there was more going on under the surface. With Mack on the other hand, the feelings showed at once, and right now his face was showing a certain amount of irritation. Bridie decided it was time she took charge before an argument broke out.
"What about that gully?" She said, pointing slightly south wards.
Lukas and Mack both turned and looked. Slightly to the south down the valley a gully led up the hillside opposite as straight as if it had been cut with a giant's knife. Stunted trees and bushes lined the course of the dry valley as it made its way upwards.
"There's cover there right enough," remarked Mack. "Thanks lass. Now how do we get down this last bit?" And he looked down the steep drop to the stream below.
"This way!" answered Luan and he set off along what was little more than a rabbit track heading obliquely down the slope in the general direction of the gully. Mack was just about to say that he would never make it down such a path when a little hand slipped inside his. He was so surprised that before he knew what he was doing he found himself being led safely downwards with little smiles and words of encouragement from Bridie.

Seven – The Fire Striker

"When you first take the path of swords, you give up something of yourself. For the way of the sword is not about individual glory, it is not about being better than others, it is not about domination. It is the about the death of self and the birth of brotherhood."

They had reached the foot of the hill and were splashing across the shallow gravel of the stream when Mack stopped suddenly.
"Look!" He pointed upstream.
Luan looked up, tense with the expectation of seeing horses and riders bearing down on them, but there was nothing there and he relaxed.
"What?" he asked.
"There again!" replied Mack.
Luan was puzzled but then, as he looked upstream, he saw a ring appear on the surface of the moving water, close to the bank about twenty yards upstream. A fish? Had Mack gone crazy?
"You two, watch the road!" and with that Mack started creeping quietly up the bank. He stopped a few feet down from the spot where the trout had shown itself and Luan watched in amazement as Mack then lay down and slowly wriggled up the bank. When he reached the spot just below the fish the old man pushed his sleeve up and then almost

imperceptibly lowered his hand and forearm into the water. He then lay absolutely still, so still that without the slow movement of the water the moment could have been frozen in time. Suddenly his arm dipped into the water and then up and out as he simultaneously rolled onto his back and something flipped into the air, flashed in the sun and then fell next him on the bank. A childish excitement took hold of Luan and he ran up the bank, aware of Bridie following close behind. Mack rolled to his feet and scooped up his catch. The trout's golden flanks were sprinkled with red spots, its jaws decorated with tiny teeth.
"Supper!" he exclaimed with a grin.
"How did you do that? It was like magic!" Luan was entranced.
"You've never seen anyone tickle trout before?" asked Mack, "anyway, I thought you were watching the road?"
Luan and Bridie looked at each other and gave a guilty shrug.
"Go on!" said Mack "I'll see if I can get a couple more"
Luan and Bridie moved off to the road as Mack started creeping up the bank.
"I'll take the North, you take the South," said Bridie and set off, leaving Luan feeling slightly pushed around. He walked about 30 paces along the track until he reached a point where the valley started to open out slightly. Reasoning that it was better to avoid being seen he moved a little off the track and into the shelter of a clump of hawthorns. To the south he could see the village, low roofs rising above the fields that surrounded it. Most of the

farming in this region was sheep and goats, but each village would have fields close by for wheat, vegetables, and sometimes the occasional cow. Luan could see no sign of life and he wondered if the villagers were in hiding from the slavers. He turned and looked back up the track but Bridie was nowhere in sight. For a moment he felt a stab of concern but then realised that she had probably had the sense to take cover just as he had. Luan turned his gaze southwards and kept watch.

His vigil didn't last long. A long, low whistle caused him to turn and he saw Mack standing with his arm raised. Luan started to jog back towards him and he saw Bridie rise up out of the long grass by the side of the track and start to make her way back. Luan stopped where the gully started up the side of the hill and waited for the other two.
"Did you get some more?" he asked as Mack and Bridie arrived.
"Two more!" confirmed Mack. "Good uns too. Should make us a nice supper if we can find a safe spot to cook them. Sure you want go up here?"
Luan looked up the gully. It was definitely manageable, there was a narrow path running up the left hand side, but it could well be steep in places.
"I still think we need to get off this track," he said, "and the sooner the better"
"Better get going then. I'll go first." Bridie grinned and then set off, Mack behind her and Luan bringing up the rear, every now and then casting worried glances behind him.

They were about half way up when his fears were realised. It was the dust of the horses' hooves that alerted him before he even heard the noise.
"Down!" he ordered. Fortunately the gully twisted at that point and they were able to view the road while remaining out of sight. All three watched as a group of riders, fur clad and armed, came into view. They were clearly looking for something, guiding their small dark coloured horses slowly along the track.

"Mountain ponies from the south," whispered Mack.
The riders paused close to where Bridie had crossed the stream and one of them got down and squatted in the dust. After a moment he stood and pointed first north and then south. He remounted and the group cantered off southwards. Luan held his breath as they reached the point where the gully started up the hill but the riders kept going and soon were out of sight.
"Whew!" he said letting his breath out. "That was close."
"They have someone who can track though," said Mack
Bridie looked at Luan "Good decision to get us off the track sword boy," she said with a smile. Luan didn't know whether to feel proud or annoyed and settled for confused.
"Let's keep going," he said, and took the lead, the others falling in behind him.

It was hard work, particularly the last hundred yards before the top, but finally the gulley opened out onto a wide, open

stretch of moorland. Mack immediately sank down onto the rough grass.
"Eeee! Bit hard on the old legs that one!" He lay back, eyes closed. Luan checked that they were not visible from the track below and then copied his example. Bridie looked at them with amusement.
"Well, while you two guard the path, I shall take a look around," and with that she was off, running lightly over the grass.

Bridie stopped to catch her breath as soon as she was out of sight. She was tired from the climb but she did not want to show any weakness in front of the others. In her brief time as a slave she had felt weak and helpless and she vowed never to feel that way again. She shuddered inside at the thought and then pushed it away, she was free now, and she was going to stay that way.

Bridie surveyed the landscape around her. To her left the ridge ran on, curving round towards the north east and undulating slightly. She could see that in the distance it climbed to a hill which to her looked man made, and Bridie decided she didn't want to go that way. In front of her the rough grasses of the moors fell away gently, splashed in autumn sunshine, and heading slightly south of east was a rough track which led down towards a small wood. In the distance beyond another ridge reared up towards the sky, and the clouds that hung above it were tinged with grey, a change in the weather was coming. The wood looked like the best chance of shelter. Happy with her choice she set off back.

When she returned Mack was still lying on his back snoring slightly but Luan was up and watching the track.

"Anything?" she asked.
Luan shook his head. "No, but I wouldn't bet on them not following. They seemed very keen to find us."
Bridie noticed that Luan said 'us' not 'you' and she thought again what an unusual boy he was. He had accepted her without question and had made no attempt to push her around, unlike most of the boys she had known. Luan turned and looked at the sky.
"We could do with some shelter," he said.
"I've found just the place," Bridie replied. "Come on!"
They shook Mack, who woke with a start, and seemed quite surprised to find himself on a hilltop. They made their way up and over the ridge and as they started down the other side they felt the first hesitant drops of rain on the wind. Just in time they reached the wood, the wind was gusting stronger and rain was starting to fall in earnest. Bridie led the way into the trees, walking into the gloom with a confidence that belied her age. The trees were mostly pines, the soft needles underfoot seemed to deaden all sound other than the wind buffeting the branches high above them.
"There!" Bridie pointed and then darted off to the left. Luan and Mack followed her to where one of the trees had fallen only to catch against another, its branches digging into the

ground to frame a natural den under the trunk.
"Careful!" warned Mack. "If it looks good to us then it would look just as good to a wolf or a bear!"
"I smell nothing," said Bridie. Luan looked at her curiously. It would never occur to him to sniff out danger. Once again he was reminded that he was far from home and this was no pretend adventure such as he used to play with his brother. This was real danger and goose bumps rose on his skin as a shiver ran down his spine.
"I'll check it out," he said, although that was the last thing he felt like doing. Slowly he edged forward, moving to the point where an opening in the branches would allow him to look inside. Getting more nervous the closer he got, the last few inches were almost unbearable and Luan felt his heart pounding as he peered round the branch and into the space beyond. To his profound relief the den was empty and Luan blew his breath out between his teeth in a long, low sigh.
"All clear," he called to the others and in a few seconds Bride and Mack joined him.

The space inside was a rough triangle, not completely enclosed but with enough branches to provide some shelter. The trunk of the fallen tree acted as a ridge pole would on a tent and the extensive tangle of twigs and leaves caught in the branches made a untidy but effective roof. It was just high enough for Bridie to stand upright, Mack and even Luan had to stoop. The floor was reasonably clear, just a few sticks and twigs among the pine needles. In the centre was a shallow pit with some fire blackened stones around

it, proof that the shelter had been used before.
"A palace fit for a king!" exclaimed Mack. "We just need the feast. Fortunately we are well provided for." He slipped his pack off his shoulder and brought out the three plump trout he had caught earlier.
"Luan! A fire if you please? I shall prepare these," and he bent down and pulled an old knife from the side of his boot.
"Better take those outside to clean them," said Bridie. "Our little home will smell bad enough without having an extra helping of fish guts."
Luan pulled a face. He wasn't overly keen on fish to begin with, still, he was hungry and he concentrated on getting a fire going. 'Better keep it small,' he said to himself as he unstrapped the sword from his back and laid it safely on the floor out of the way. 'We'll be in a right mess if the whole tree blazes up.' He opened his own pack and took out his axe. It was an unusual tool with a short wooden handle polished with use. The iron head was small with a sharp blade on one side and a solid squared off lump on the other. Luan had picked up the tool in the blacksmith's on the day before he left home and even in the short time he had been travelling it had been amazingly useful. Now he used the blade to dig out the fire pit some more and then he covered the floor of the pit with twigs in a criss-cross pattern. On top of that he piled up as many small dry twigs as possible, leaving a hole at the side in which to insert the tinder. Then he used the axe blade to chop up a decent pile of sticks which he put to one side before taking from his pack a small oiled pouch. A curious Bridie looked on as he opened

it to reveal two strange looking objects, some blackened broken twigs and some dried grass.
"What's that?" she asked.
"My fire making kit. Have you never seen one?"
"No," said Bridie
"How do you light a fire then?" Luan looked astonished.
"We don't," said Bridie defensively. "We just don't let them go out."
"What about when you travel?"
Bridie thought for a moment. "Well, all our travelling is by boat. Not a good idea, lighting a fire on a boat."
Luan considered this and decided it made sense. Then another question occurred to him. "So what about cooking?"
"Salt fish and black bread is what you take on a sea voyage. No cooking needed!" Now it was Bridie's turn to be surprised.
"Wait," said Luan, "You've never lit a fire?"
"And you've never been on a boat?" replied Bridie. She sounded worried, less confident. They looked at each other afresh, both suddenly feeling that a gulf had opened between them. After a moment Luan smiled. "Tell you what," he said. "I'll show you how to make a fire, then one day you can teach me about boats." Bridie smiled her agreement and Luan proceeded to explain step by step how to light the fire, naming the flint, the iron firestriker and the tinder and letting Bridie have a go at striking sparks herself. Bridie was fascinated by the firestriker. She loved the shape, the way the shaft where the flint struck elongated

and curved over on itself to give a finger grip. This was not an unusual feature but the smith who had crafted this piece had then worked it unto the shape of a dragon's neck and at the end a likeness of the dragon's head so that when the sparks flew it looked as if the dragon was breathing fire. She held the object in her hand, feeling the cold and the weight of it. Iron was rarely used in her country and she found it amazing that the people of the kingdom treated it as just part of the everyday way of things. Finally she handed it back to Luan who had carefully shaken a few of the charcoal twigs onto a piece of bark. He held the iron in his left hand close to the bark and the flint in his right. Then with three sharp blows he sent a shower of sparks onto the blackened sticks and immediately blew so that the sparks caught and began to glow red. A pinch of dried grass and another breath and smoke began to curl up. Another pinch of tinder and one more blow and a flame caught. Luan pushed the whole thing into the centre of his carefully prepared fireplace and knelt to blow carefully through the base, trying to keep a constant flow of air. The smoke thickened and the dry sticks began to crackle as the flame caught. Luan sat up, face red with the effort and then he sat carefully feeding the flame. Bridie looked on, feeling as if she had witnessed a miracle.

Eight – Luan's Sword

"The swords we carry are our inheritance and our gift. The time for which we wield them is just one chapter in their history. While we hold them they feel part of us, alive, an extension of our limbs. But then we pass them on to the next generation, so that they live on after we have fought our battles."

Mack woke early the next morning. He was cold and stiff. "Getting too old for all this nonsense," he muttered to himself. Even as he said it he knew it wasn't true, it was just automatic old man grumbling. In truth he felt younger than he had in years. "That's what a sense of freedom does for you," he thought. For a moment he felt a pang of guilt at leaving old Brinna, but he pushed it aside. He had given her a lot more than he had taken and that seemed a fair deal to him. Mack made his way out of the rough shelter, taking care not to disturb the others. He looked down at them, Bridie looking very young, her dark hair falling over her face, Luan clutching the sword as if even in sleep it defined his life. Pushing his way out into the wood, he marvelled at the stillness. The storm of the previous night had passed and sunlight was breaking through the trees, illuminating patches of ground so that they glowed, contrasting strongly with the shadows that still remained. Mack reached the edge of the wood and made his way along the track they had followed the night before. He looked for any sign of the previous day's pursuit; but the whole of the open moor seemed uninhabited. Mack was alone underneath the dome of the sky and he revelled in the feeling.

A few yards away the track was cut by a narrow channel where a trickle of water made its way downhill. Mack followed the fledgling stream back up the hill until he came to the place where the water bubbled up from the rock into a small pool. He knelt and drank, enjoying the cool, slightly peaty taste of the water. Then he rinsed out and filled his flask before splashing water on his face. Suddenly there was a noise behind him and Mack whipped round, a hand reaching for the knife in his boot. The sheep took a step back, as if affronted by Mack's reception, and then nibbled a piece of grass, all the while watching carefully with its big soulful eyes. Mack smiled "Sorry old girl," he said. "You had me goin' a bit there." He stood up, looking around carefully, the incident leaving him with a sense of being watched. Mack no longer felt carefree; instead he had the feeling that there could be an assailant behind every rock or bush. His thoughts turned to Bridie and Luan, asleep on their own and quickly he began to make his way back.

He found Luan sitting outside the shelter.
"Bridie's still asleep," he said.
"No she's not!" Bridie followed close behind the retort, looking tousled and rubbing her eyes as she made her way

out of the shelter.
"I found some water," said Mack, sitting down and handing round his flask. "Now," he said when they had both drank, "I think we need to make some plans. Where are we going?"
"I have to go to the guild house at Sanlynn," said Luan, "but I think we she try to help Bridie return to her people."
Bridie snorted. "That's the last thing I want."
Luan was surprised. "But you were taken from them!"
"No," said Bridie. "I ran away. It was after that I was caught by those thugs."
"Why did you run away?"
"I'm not sure that's your business!" She gave Luan a long look. "Let's just say there is more than one sort of slavery."
"So you're not going back? Where will you go?" Luan was having difficulty grasping the idea that a girl may strike out on her own. In his village it would have been unthinkable. Yet again he reminded himself how little he knew of the wider world.
Bridie smiled at his confusion. "Thanks to you I am free, and I intend to keep it that way. But at the same time I know it is safer to travel with others. As for where I go, one place is as good as another to me. Maybe I will come with you, keep you out of trouble!"
Mack nodded. He understood Bridie's motives completely, his weren't so different. "I too will come with you. I need a town where I can ply my trade, and Sanlynn will serve as well as any other. But we must take care, it is likely to take two weeks on foot and the kingdom is not as safe as it once

was. We will need food and water, and the means to protect ourselves as well as we can. We might run into the slavers again, and there are others who might well think that an old man and two children make an easy target."
Luan looked up and nodded. He had already realised there was a lot more to Mack than met the eye. Here was another side of the old man, strategic and responsible. Mack smiled back. "Maybe it's about time you learned how to use that sword you been carrying around. Come on!"
He got up and made his way to a clearing, the children following. They watched as Mack made his way around the trees checking the branches that were close to the ground.
"Here," he said, "this would make a good staff. Luan, you got that axe?"
Luan handed it over and watched as Mack cut two branches from the tree and trimmed them of leaves and twigs. Each was about two inches in diameter but of different lengths, one was about a man’s height, the other about half that. Mack handed the shorter to Luan.
"What's this?" asked Luan.
"Your sword, for now," replied Mack. "I'm not letting you near me with the real thing until I know you've got the hang of it. I'd like to keep all my body parts exactly where they are thank you."
Bridie sniggered. This looked like it might be fun to watch.
"Why is your stick longer than mine?" Luan sounded slightly petulant.
"It's not a stick, it's a staff, a quarter staff some would call it. And a useful weapon it is too for someone as knows

what they're doing. Yours is a practice sword so it's about the right length. Now come on, have at me!"
Luan paused. He didn't really feel like attacking Mack, and with Bridie watching he felt awkward with it. Still, they had to start somewhere so he held the 'sword' out in front of him and then he stepped forward bringing the sword up and then arcing down towards Mack's head.
Crack! Quick as a flash Mack brought the staff up horizontally to block Luan's blow. Then before the boy could recover he whipped his left hand down so that the end of the staff hit Luan on the right leg just below the knee. Then his right arm shot out like a punch, landing a blow to the chest that put Luan flat on his back.
"Oof!" Luan felt the breath shoot out of him and he lay, winded, on his back. He could hear Bridie giggling. Gritting his teeth he took Mack's proffered hand and hauled himself back to his feet.
"Never commit yourself to a single blow," said Mack. "Try to anticipate, think two or three strokes ahead. Now try again."
This time Luan feinted the blow to the head but then jumped back a step and swung in a low arc to block Mack's attack on his legs. Unfortunately as soon as he stepped back Mack simply slid his right hand down the staff to meet his left and used the length of the staff to deal a sharp crack on the boy's head. Luan sat down with a bump, his head ringing and not just with Bridie's laughter. He stared at her until she stopped, choking off the giggles with a hand over her mouth.

"Just wait until it's your turn!" Luan said. "Then we'll see who's laughing!"
"Oh no, not me!" said Bridie. "I don't need a stick to defend myself. Watch!"
Luan and Mack watched intrigued as Bridie undid the leather thongs that she used as a belt. Leaving one band in place she unthreaded the two others and then shook them out so that it was obvious that they joined at a canvas pouch.
"A slingshot!" said Mack, his voice tinged with awe.
"Exactly!" replied Bridie and she stooped and picked up a stone the size of a pheasant's egg. She placed it in the canvas pouch and then began to swing the slingshot, round and round, faster and faster until she let go one of the thongs. The stone flew out and shot through the wood to smash a chunk of bark from a tree thirty paces away.
"That's amazing!" Luan stared at the young girl.
"I know!" said Bridie with a grin. "Now you boys get on with playing with sticks and I'll go and collect some stones."
Luan watched her scamper off through the wood with a feeling that he was the least useful member of the party. Suddenly he whipped a blow towards Mack's legs, then, swinging his body round, he shoulder charged, slamming his elbow into the old man's stomach. Mack staggered back but then started to bring his staff up in a counter attack only to stop dead as he felt the end of Luan's sword touch the side of his neck. Luan stood there, arm outstretched, with a massive grin on his face. Mack acknowledged the boy's

success with a nod and he stepped back.
"Well done lad! I see you know the value of surprise."
"When your only brother is older and bigger than you, you've got to be sneaky!" replied Luan.
"We might make a fighter of you yet," said Mack. "Now, defend yourself!" and he launched a flurry of blows.

After half an hour Mack called a halt and they sat down on a log to catch their breath. In the first ten bouts Luan had 'won' precisely two, in the last ten he had won five. Bridie had re-joined them after about twenty minutes and she had been delighted to see Luan giving almost as good as he got.
"Right," said Mack when he had caught his breath. "Better have a look at that sword."
Luan picked up the sword and grasped the hilt. The blade slid from the scabbard with a whisper, Luan was surprised at how little effort it took to draw. The gleaming metal shone in the sun, the surface of the blade free of rust and dirt yet Luan could see the faint tracing of swirls and marks formed in the swords forging. He remembered Marius showing him the sword and how in his childish way Luan had said that it looked like the blade had feathers and Marius had laughed at the description.
"It's beautiful!" said Bridie, her eyes big and round, staring in childish amazement.
"Moralean iron!" Exclaimed Mack "In many a long year I have never seen its like!"
"What do you mean?" asked Luan.

"The swords of legend, brought back to mortal lands from the islands of the otherworld." Bride stared in awe as she continued. "Forged in dragon fire, they bring power to those that wield them and are deadly to hags, ghouls and other monsters that cannot be harmed by normal blades." She stopped and looked at Luan "How come you've got one then?"
Luan felt vaguely offended. "It was my uncle's, he was a Klaideem. It's not magic or anything though, just a sword."
"It's not just a sword" retorted Bridie "I have seen all the warriors of my tribe arrayed for battle, none had a sword such as this. The swords of my people are shorter, shaped like this" and she used both hands to trace out a slim leaf shape.
"Bronze swords," said Mack, "such as the northern tribes use." He paused and looked at her appraisingly. "Which tribe are you from Bridie?"
"The Tribe of the Bani-Tivar," she answered proudly. Mack gave a sharp intake of breath.
Luan was feeling lost again. "You're not from the Kingdom then?"
"No" said Bridie again with pride in her voice "My tribe rules the northern lands. We live free and bow the knee to no one!"
"You're a long way from home girl!" said Mack. "Did the slavers bring you all this way?"
Bridie nodded. "I had been away one night when they caught me. Then twelve days of travel, from the shores of the northern sea, through the mountains and across the

plains, always heading southwards."
"As I thought," said Mack, "they only had one destination in mind."
"The Pireacht Empire," said Luan
"Exactly," agreed Mack, "they would get a good price in the southern cities for a young girl like you, Bridie."
Bridie sniffed. "Well they haven't got me now and I'm assuming we're not just going to sit here and wait until they find us again!"
"You're right," said Luan, sliding the sword home in the scabbard and standing up, "we should go."
"Wait." Mack held out his hands in a calming gesture. "Not so fast! Are we agreed we are heading for Sanlynn?" The others nodded their agreement. "Then the way is east, following the same path. One more thing, Luan! Put the sword on as you normally wear it."
The sword was too long for Luan to wear at his waist so he had taken to wearing it on his back with the baldric, the leather belt from which the sword hung, across his chest. He did so now, slipping it over one arm and his head so that it hung diagonally with the hilt over his left shoulder.
"Now draw," Mack instructed.
Luan reached up with his right hand and started to pull the sword from the scabbard. It came easily enough at first but he soon found that the movement was awkward to the point of impossible as he tried to straighten his arm. With a feeling of dismay he gave up and pushed the sword back.
"As I thought," said Mack. "Don't worry, I have a plan. Half undo the buckle on the baldric. Don't worry, the

weight of the sword will keep it tight."
Luan did as he was asked, pulling the leather tongue from the buckle.
"Now," continued Mack "as you draw with your right hand, undo the buckle with your left and just let it go."
Luan tried it and found that as he drew the sword the scabbard fell to land on the floor behind him leaving the sword free.
"Excellent! Now try it again as if for real."
Luan re-buckled the baldric, replaced the sword and repositioned the whole thing on his back. Then he tried the manoeuvre again, this time finishing in the stance that Mack had showed him. One foot in front of the other, elbows in towards his hips, the sword in both hands pointing forwards with the tip raised.
"Now you look like a warrior, Luan!" Bridie's words were sincere. Luan tried to keep a serious face such as a warrior would have but then blushed and grinned.

Nine – The Standing Stone

"When you follow the path of swords there is no telling where it will lead. Do not be surprised if it leads you to other tribes, other countries, even other worlds..."

The path led downhill. In the distance they could see the landscape changing, the hills and moors of their journey softening into a gentle undulation. They could see that the path was heading into a valley; the small trickle of water where they had filled their flasks was one of a number of tributaries that seemed eager to join together, splashing over rocks and carving out earth banks as if practising for more serious erosion that would take place later. Viewed from the moor the valley looked like the indentation of a branch pushed into soft dough, the hard edges of the fledgling valleys rounded off by a covering of light green ferns. The going was easy as they walked single file along the narrow path and for the most part they avoided talk and concentrated solely on the task of reducing the miles between them and their destination. "This is companionship," thought Luan as they walked and he considered that he was lucky to fall in with Mack and Bridie, even though he really knew very little about them. This prompted a question and Luan caught up with Mack to ask it.
"Why did you act so shocked when Bridie told you what tribe she was from?"

Mack stopped and turned round for long enough to give Luan a warning glance.
"Maybe you should ask her," he said.
Luan hesitated, balancing the possibility of upsetting someone against his overwhelming curiosity. It wasn't long before he gave in and Mack shrugged as Luan pushed past him and ran to catch up with Bridie. The track had widened slightly and he was able walk next to her, occasionally ducking under branches and pushing away ferns as they made their way into the small valley.
"Tell me something about your tribe," he said.
"What do you want to know?" Bridie replied.
"Why is it called the Bani-Tivar? What does it mean?"
Bridie stopped and turned to look at him.
“Don’t you know?”
Luan shrugged and shook his head.
“You might prefer not to know,” she warned.
“Really?” Luan smiled. “You’re going to have to tell me now.”
“Well don’t say I didn’t warn you!” Bridie smiled and they continued down the path.
"The lands of my people lie far to the north," she began. "We live on the shore of the great sea where the mountains meet the waves. We have no cities as such, but in settlements scattered along the inlets that the sea has cut into the land. In each one stands the hall of an Alfihar, a warleader and around the hall are the houses of his men. We are people of the sea and the Alfihar's pride is his ship, crewed by his war band, free men who have sworn to serve

him. The ships serve in three ways. Mostly they're just used for fishing, which is a bit dull even when hunting seals and other creatures of the deep."
"Sounds pretty exciting to me!" interrupted Luan. Bridie laughed and continued.
"Well it can be, especially in bad weather when the waves boom against the hull of the ship and the wind sings in the rigging. But what is really exciting is when the fishing nets are brought ashore and the boat is rigged for war. It's a fine sight when the shields of the war band crown the sides with colour and the flag of the Bani-Tivar flies proudly from the mast top."
"So do you fight battles at sea?" asked Luan, trying to imagine it.
"Sometimes," Bridie answered, "but mostly the men go raiding up and down the coast. Generally they head east, to the wild uncivilised lands."
Luan thought that Bridie's homeland sounded wild and uncivilised enough, but thought better of saying so.
"You said there were three purposes for the ships?"
Bridie paused and then continued. "The third is a duty. A sacred duty given to our tribe many lifetimes ago. Do you not know what it is?"
"No," said Luan.
"We are the boatmen of the dead. In your tongue Bani-Tivar means Death-God."
Luan stopped and looked at her. Bridie looked back, her eyes serious. Luan felt the hairs stand up on the back of his neck. He swallowed and cleared his throat, his mouth

suddenly dry. They started walking again and Bridie continued.
"If you sail north over the sea, after two days and nights you arrive at an empty land. It is fair and green but nothing lives there, no birds, no animals and no people. No one has set foot there and returned to tell the tale. When our tribe first came from the east their small fleet of ships was blown off course by a storm and they landed there. It is said that at first they thought to stay and claim the country for their own but in the depths of the first night they heard a roaring coming down from the north. A chill wind blew and frost began to form on the ground and the branches of the trees. Then in a cloud of snow and darkness a great ice bear appeared. A fearful beast as high as the tree tops with great claws that gouged the ground as it walked. All the people of the tribe fell to the ground in fear and waited for death for no one could fight such a beast. Then their leader, Alfihar, looked about and saw his people cowering around him and he stood and shouted a great challenge. The giant creature reached out its claw to crush him but Alfihar shouted "Stop! Great Bear, you are mighty indeed and we know you can destroy us with one swipe of your mighty claw, yet let us live and we will worship you and serve you with honour." The beast paused and then spoke with a voice like the rumbling of thunder. "I am Bani-Tivar, the Lord of Death! What have I to do with honour?" Alfihar raised his voice and shouted again and said "But there is honour in death, if a man dies bravely, for his brother, or his wife or his child" And then the wind dropped and the

cloud of darkness became light and before their eyes the great bear transformed and shrank until it resembled the form of a man of great beauty and his body was like gold and silver. "So be it," said The Lord of Death. "I will be your God and you will be my people and you will serve me until the end of days. But I tell you truthfully you may not dwell in the Land of the Dead and remain alive. So I will send you to go and dwell on the south shore of this sea and your sacred duty will be to ferry the souls of the dead from that land to this" Then he directed the tribe to sail southwards, and he made a fair wind blow their ships until they came to the land where they now live. And the tribe took the name of the Bani-Tivar after their God and their leaders have been called the Alfihar in honour of the first leader ever since."

"I don't know what to say!" said Luan. "That's the most amazing story I've ever heard."

"That's not all," replied Bridie, and she stopped and lowered her voice. "Sometimes at midnight, in the dark of the moon a bell sounds in each village. At that signal each Alfihar alone goes to ready his boat. The sea grows still and the wind dies away, and then a mist flows slowly down from the land. As the mist grows closer they say you can see glimpses of people and hear voices whisper like the wind in dry grass. The mist flows over the sea and onto the boat and grows still. Then a breeze comes from the south and the boats move smoothly over a sea like glass. When the boats reach that empty land that lies to the north of the great sea, the voices in the mist rise again in expectation

and as the boats touch shore the souls of the dead flow onto the land like a tide. Then the boats return, higher in the water now they are not laden with their dread cargo. And even though it is at least two days and nights sailing to cross the sea in ordinary times, the dark journey is made there and back in a single night!"
Once again Luan felt the tension between his own down to earth common sense and the part of him that responded to Bridie's story. It sounded so fantastical and yet he could tell that Bridie believed every word she said.

They had reached a point where the gully widened out. The small stream they had been following downhill dropped over a small fall to join with a larger stream that ran down from their right. They were in a narrow steep sided valley, its floor scattered with boulders and rocks and its sides lined with ferns and tangled thickets of trees. Luan and Bridie stopped and waited for Mack to catch up, taking the opportunity to drink from the clear water of the stream.

There was a wider path that ran down the valley on the other side of the stream and Luan decided to wade across to it. About half way across the stream divided and ran around a large stone standing in the river. Luan stopped, curious about a strange hole that went right through the stone about a foot from the top. He stooped and peered through and was surprised to see he had a clear view down the valley and out onto the plains beyond. He stood and walked round to the downstream side and peered through the hole in the other direction. There, perfectly framed, was an earth mound on the top of the ridge. "This stone must have been set here on purpose," thought Luan,, "I wonder why?" He walked around to the upstream side again and placed his hand in the hole. Suddenly Luan felt again the dizziness and sense of discontinuity that he had felt when he stepped onto the burial mound. He staggered, gripping the stone for support and called out, but his voice sounded strange and weak. He felt sick and fell to his knees in the stream, letting go of the stone as he did so. As before the feeling passed as quickly as it came, but when Luan looked up the world had changed.

When Luan was very young, a troop of travelling players had performed in his father's hall. As Luan watched their dramas unfold, the exaggerated movements, the louder than natural voices, the make up sharply defining the faces, and the brightly painted scenery had made him feel the real world to be a pale shadow that was slipping away from him. Luan had been terrified and the grotesque images of the players had haunted his dreams for months. Now, as he looked up, the same feeling took hold of him and with it came the fear. He looked about wildly; the sky was more blue, the grass a deeper shade of green, the sound of birds overhead and the stream around his feet clearer and more resonant. He looked back for Bridie and Mack, panic rising within him. At first he thought them gone, but then he realised that he could see their shadowy forms, pale and

indistinct. They seemed to be moving unnaturally quickly and with a burst of insight he realised that for him time had slowed down. It was then that he heard the music. Coming from behind him and upstream was a voice lifted in song. Multi toned, melodious and deep, the sound immediately quelled the fear that Luan felt and a sense of calm and wonder overtook him. He turned, and there walking down the track towards him was a band of warriors such as Luan had never seen before. They were pale skinned and fair haired and unclothed but for short kilts of leather. Not much taller than Luan, their skins were adorned with intricate patterns, each torso an individual labyrinth of whorls and lines. They each carried a spear and a long knife at the waist and their voices were raised in song. At first Luan thought they could not see him because they showed no sign of being aware of his presence. Then as they reached the point where he stood, the singing stopped. Luan felt the hairs on his neck begin to rise again but still the warriors paid him no heed until the last one, on the point of passing by, turned and spoke.
"Hail sword brother! Long has it been since one of the Klaideem stepped between the worlds. What news of the land of the young?"
Luan was almost too tongue tied to speak, yet he was scared to remain silent.
"I, I'm sorry," he stuttered, "I don't know where I am."
The warrior looked at him closely. Luan was acutely aware of the scrutiny. There was something ancient about those eyes even though the face seemed youthful.

"I see now that I was mistaken," the warrior said. "To one such as I, all of you look young. You did not mean to cross over did you?"
"No!" Luan replied. “What do you mean 'one such as you'? Who are you? And where am I?"
The stranger smiled. "To answer those questions would be a long tale indeed. My name is Zand, and let us just say that long ages ago in your time I crossed over from your world to this, that you call the spirit world. Now I must go and join my brothers in the hunt, and you must go back. This is a perilous place, and I shudder to think what would happen if the being that we track found you."
"But I don't know how to get back!"
"Never fear," said Zand with a smile. "I will send you on your way," and with that he stepped forward and put his hand on Luan’s forehead.

Ten – The Hunters of the Moon

"On the journey you will face many enemies. They come in different guises. But there is one foe that you will carry with you wherever you go, whoever you fight. Before you face your enemy in battle, you must face fear."

Often when Luan woke he could remember his dreams, sharply defined images of battle and conflict, groups of riders or spearman starkly illuminated as if by lightening flash. These he had become accustomed to since he was a child. But sometimes he would wake knowing that he had been dreaming but with no recollection, just a strong feeling of disconnection that would stay with him all day.

Waking on the banks of the stream, he had the same sort of feeling, coupled with an awareness that the world was somehow lessened to his senses.
"Luan! Luan!"
His name. He remembered now. He remembered everything.
"Bridie?" His voice sounded like it belonged to someone else. He opened his eyes. "What happened?"
"You're awake!" The relief in Bridie's voice was tangible. "Mack! Come quick!"
There was a rustle in the bushes downstream and Mack appeared, running back up the bank.
"What happened?" He looked and sounded angry. "You've

been gone an hour! Where have you been?"
Luan didn't know what to say. An hour? It had only seemed like minutes to him. Would his friends believe him? And if they did would they treat him differently? Luan suddenly realised that his clothes were soaking wet and his head hurt. He put his hand to his forehead and it came away red with blood.
"I, I hit my head," he said and added the lie, "I can't really remember."
"You disappeared," said Bridie, her eyes large. "We didn't know where you were. At first we didn't worry, but then when you didn't come back we started searching, I went upstream and Mack down." She pointed down the valley. "I was just coming back when I heard a cry and a splash. I ran the last bit and you were just pulling yourself out of the stream. And then you collapsed!" Luan could see a tear starting to form in the corner of Bridie's eye. Then speaking almost to herself she said "Don't worry, you're ok now," and pulling her sleeve down over her palm she began to wipe the blood from his forehead. Luan, surprised by the sudden tenderness, opened his mouth and then, with a stab of guilt, closed it again. Looking up, Luan caught Mack's expression and knew that the old man was not so easily distracted.
"Later," Luan mouthed. Mack looked at him keenly for a moment and then turned away with a nod.

They crossed the stream and Luan noticed that both Bridie and Mack gave the stone a wide berth without seeming to notice it. At first the path twisted and wound around rocks then at times climbed almost to the lip of valley so that they could see the stream sparkling below them in the afternoon sun, which, he was very pleased to find, was starting to dry Luan's clothes. They walked without speaking, pushing through the ferns which sprouted in clumps from between the rocks and scrambling across the gullies that every so often cut the side of the valley. After a while the valley started to open out some more and the going got easier. Even then they walked in silence, each occupied by their own thoughts.

They camped for the night in a copse of hazel trees that grew where a small gully ran down to meet the river. Luan lit a small fire over which they cooked a rabbit, brought down by Bridie's slingshot. They were all tired after a long march and Bridie soon fell asleep leaving Mack and Luan sitting, watching over the fire. It was Mack who broke the silence.
"Are you going to tell me then?"
"I don't know." Luan wasn't sure how to explain that to talk about it would be to admit that something had happened. To finally give up the internal struggle that had been taking place within him since he left home. Luan looked up at the stars splashed brightly across the sky and suddenly realised that this was all part of his journey. He had given up the safety of home and taken to the hard life of the road understanding that it was an essential step in following his path. Now he realised that he had to step out of the security

of his scepticism and accept that there was far more to the world than he had ever believed possible. He looked at the old man slouched opposite him, face dark in the flickering light of the flames and decided it was time.
"You remember when we were at the burial mound and I stepped off the path?" Luan began, "I said I tripped."
Mack's eyes were locked on Luan "No trip that, I knew it at the time."
Luan shook his head. "No, but what happened was so strange that I was too scared to admit it, even to myself, and then today..." His voice tailed off and he stared into the fire. Mack looked at the young boy, sensing the turmoil inside him.
"You stepped into the other world didn't you?"
"Yes." Luan glanced up at Mack across the fire and suddenly the words started to come. He let it all out, the strange sensations, the brightness and most of all the meeting with the unworldly Zand. Mack sat silently throughout, his eyes glinting brightly as they reflected the glow of the fire. When Luan had finished talking there was a long pause, punctuated only by the occasional crack of the embers. When Mack finally spoke it was so quiet that Luan could hardly hear him.
"The Hunters of the Moon."
"What?"
"The men you describe are the Hunters of the Moon. I recognise them from the old songs."
"What old songs? And how can you hunt the moon?" Luan was tired, and still wrestling with his own confusion.

Mack looked across the fire and smiled. "Listen," he said and began to sing.

The grass was green in the morning of the world
And dew wet the feet of the hunters of the dawn
As they tracked the deer through sunlit trees
And fished for salmon in the clear bright streams

No king had they or need of one
No house or farm to hold them down.
All the land was theirs from the hills to the sea
And they owned it not but hunted free.

The hunters were of one with the land
Mother and father it was to them
But then came the tribes from the furthest east
And shattered the hunters gentle peace.

He broke off, and picking up a stick he leaned forward to poke the fire. A shower of sparks whirled up in the breeze, momentarily casting light on the branches above them.
"That is the start of it. One of the oldest songs it is, telling of the first days before the tribes came to the land. It tells the story of the hunters, who saw their land being tamed and broken and knew it meant the end of their time. So they chose to leave the land they loved and walk the spirit world instead."
"And I met them," responded Luan.
"I believe so."

"So why do you call them the hunters of the moon?"
Mack glanced up at the branches silhouetted against the stars.
"The final part of the legend is that when the night is clear and the moon lights up the land, then the hunters return to walk the land they loved and so they are called the Hunters of the Moon."

That night Luan dreamt he was one of the hunters, spear in hand in the moonlight, bare feet walking the high places of the land.

The next morning dawned grey with drizzle, and they set off without delay. Autumn was passing quickly and it was only a matter of time before the worsening weather started to delay them. Half a day’s march saw them reach the mouth of the valley where the track they followed joined a heavily used road. Behind them the land rose to the moors and in front of them it opened out in a wide shallow bowl of gently rolling farmland dotted with copses of trees. Here and there they could see smoke that indicated settlements. The stream they followed was now a small river with a wide shallow ford where it met the road and it was here they stopped.
"Which way now?" asked Bridie.
Mack looked up trying to gauge the position of the sun, and shook his head.
"As far as I can tell this road runs north to south, and we've been heading east but I can’t be sure."

"Sanlynn lies to the East." Luan looked out over the fields, "But I can see no obvious path."
"Cut across country?" suggested Bridie.
Mack grimaced. "Hard going even across farmland! Stick to the road until we come to a path going our way, that's what I think."
Luan wasn't sure. "On the road we're out in the open, very easy to find."
Worry shot across Bridie's face. "You think they're still after us?"
"I think we have to assume so, at least..." Luan stopped mid-sentence, his voice tailing off as he stared at the three riders who had just walked their horses into the road some distance to the north.
"Well, I think that answers that question." Mack had seen them too.
The slavers seemed in no hurry. They seemed to be waiting to see what their quarry would do.
"Why are they just sitting there?" Bridie asked the question for all three of them.
"And where are the others?" added Mack.
"That's it," said Luan, "they're in no hurry because they know they've got us trapped. There must be other small bands like this one, probably one to the south and others searching the moor"
"Then there are only two possibilities," said Mack grimly, "surrender, or fight"
Something suddenly snapped inside Luan as the frustration he felt at being pursued boiled up inside him. He reached

his right hand over his shoulder to grip the sword while the left undid the buckle at his chest.
"Looks like we're fighting then," observed Mack.
Bridie whooped with excitement as Mack hefted his staff.
Up the track, the three riders also began to prepare themselves. One, armed with a spear, stood up in his stirrups to look first northwards and then south while the others hefted heavy clubs. The spearman pointed and then all three set off at a walk.

Luan looked at the men who would have no hesitation in maiming or killing him and felt a tight ball of fear growing in his stomach. His heart pounded and he could feel the muscles across his shoulders and in his arms begin to tighten, pumping with blood as his body readied itself for action. Luan struggled to swallow as his mouth went suddenly dry and to his heightened perceptions time seemed to slow down. To his left Mack stepped forward to the edge of the ford.
"Take them at the edge, don't let them onto dry land." The old man's voice was raw but steady.
Luan swallowed again and took three steps, halting just short of the swiftly flowing water. He pushed his left foot forward holding the sword in the position that Mack called 'guard', both hands on the hilt, elbows tucked in, the blade pointing forwards and up. Up ahead the spearman barked an order and all three horses broke into a canter.

The image seared itself into Luan's memory. A frozen

tableau that he knew would stay with him for the rest of his life. The three horsemen, hard eyed, grimacing, left hands clutching reigns as their heels kicked against the horses' flanks. Closer they came, cloaked in rough furs, their bearded faces grimy from a life on the road. The horses in fluid motion, breath snorting, their drumming hooves kicking up the dirt.

The spell was broken by a whirring and a shout from behind him and a stone flew hard and fast from Bridie's sling. Flying true it thumped into the chest of the foremost horse causing it to rear up, pawing the air with a shrill neigh. The horseman was thrown backwards and he struggled to stay in control as the horse span in a tight circle before galloping off down the road, its rider hanging on desperately, half out of the saddle. Luan just had time to register Bridie's yell of triumph before the remaining two riders reached the river and splashed into the shallow water. The spearman was heading straight for Luan. To his left Luan was dimly aware of Mack shouting and lunging with his staff as the other rider spurred his horse forward with a ferocious swing of his club. Then the spearman was on him, half standing in the stirrups as he thrust down at Luan. Seeing the blow coming, Luan swayed to the right and caught the spear shaft on his sword blade. To his surprise and delight the sword sheared straight through the haft, the spearhead falling to the dirt. He span to the right aiming a backhand blow at the rider above him, but the momentum of the horse carried the slaver away and the sword hummed through empty air. The rider continued down the road intent on Bridie, who turned and ran. Luan charged after, sprinting to catch up. He glanced over his shoulder, hoping that Mack didn't need his help, and saw that the old man had managed to knock his opponent out of the saddle. In front of him the slaver reached Bride and leaned out of the saddle trying to grab the young girl by the hair. She screamed and darted to one side, eluding the man’s grasp but then slipping as she tried to run back towards Luan. The horseman shouted in triumph as he wheeled his horse back to the prone girl but the delay was just enough time for Luan to get there. He leapt over Bridie and slashed his sword upwards desperately trying to defend them both. Luan felt the shock down his arm as the blade connected and then his ears were filled with an animal scream as the horse reacted to the savage cut down the side of its head. It reared, hooves flailing, blood spraying, and then fell to one side, pitching the rider to the ground with a thud. Luan grabbed Bridie and dragged her clear as the horse continued to roll, its hoof catching the slaver's head with a sickening crack. Then it was up and galloping away down the track leaving its rider's lifeless body behind.

There was no time to celebrate victory. Luan looked round wildly to where Mack still struggled with the other rider. To his dismay Luan saw that the third rider had regained control of his mount and was galloping back down the track towards them. Mack shouted with triumph as he landed a blow that knocked his foe's club from his hand and sent the man staggering backwards, his arm hanging limply at his side. But even as Mack stepped forward to deliver a final blow the remaining slaver swept up behind him, beating down with his club. The full momentum of the horse and rider sent Mack flying to land in a crumpled heap on the road. Luan ran forward, raising his sword, determined to help his friend, but the slavers weren't interested in continuing the fight. With one man down, another injured and a well-armed, determined foe still to face the last rider pulled his companion up behind him and fled.

Eleven - Aftermath

"As you make this journey you must start to recognise and develop your strength. Not only physical strength, although this is important, but also the inner strength to step forward into the unknown, to carry on when all seems lost, and to support those that are not as strong as you."

Just for a moment a feeling of elation filled Luan as he stood listening to the hoof beats fade away. He had survived! Then Bridie moaned and Luan ran to her.
"Are you alright?"
Bridie sat up, shaking her head.
"Ow! Think I banged my head. Nothing serious though."
She took the hand that Luan offered her and climbed gingerly to her feet.
"Where's Mack?" Bridie looked around and saw Mack's still form. Her face suddenly contorted in grief and she dashed to his side, Luan at her heels. Tears started in her eyes as she struggled to get him onto his back. Together the two youngsters managed to turn him and Bridie searched frantically for a pulse.
"He's alive." Relief filled Bridie's voice.
Together, Bridie and Luan did their best to clean the old man up. His face and hands were badly cut from his fall and they washed them with water from the river. As far as they could tell there were no broken bones and his breathing, although shallow, was regular. Beyond that they

knew only that despite their best attempts he wasn't waking up.

After an unsuccessful attempt to get Mack to drink, the water just pouring out the side of his mouth, Luan stood and looked up and down the road, worried that the slavers would come back and find them helpless. The body of the horseman lay a short distance away, head at an unnatural angle, neck clearly broken by force of the horse's hoof. Luan suddenly started to shiver uncontrollably and he sank to his knees as a wave of nausea broke over him.
"Luan? Are you hurt?" He was aware of Bridie stooping over him.
"I killed him!" The words seemed inadequate for the enormity of the deed. He felt the soft touch of Bridie's hand on the back of his head, and then her hands grabbed his upper arms and pulled him to his feet. When she spoke her voice was hard.
"Yes, you did. And if you hadn't he would have killed you without a thought, and Mack, and he would have sold me into slavery. He was an evil man who lived off the misery of others. I'm glad he's dead!"
Luan looked at her, strong spirit in such a slight body.
"Still," he said, "it doesn't feel right"
"That's because you are good." Bride's fierce expression softened and she smiled. "My people say that when you face your first enemy in battle you become a man. You won your first fight and now..."
She stepped back and raised her arm across her chest, fist

clenched in a formal gesture.
"Hail warrior of the Bani-Tivar! This day you become my brother!" Bridie caught sight of the bewildered expression on her friend's face and giggled, dispelling the mock seriousness of the moment.
"What are you doing?" asked Luan, bemused by her behaviour.
"It's the welcome to the clan. There's loads more of it but I can't remember."
"What happens then?"
"The new warrior has the Bani-Tivar tattooed on his chest and the victory mark on his arm."
Luan thought that sounded painful. "Let's skip that bit," he suggested.

Luan looked around, trying to formulate a plan. The slavers would be back, so staying on the road was not an option but with Mack unconscious getting off it was nearly impossible. Then a movement a little way off caught his eye.
"Look after Mack," he said over his shoulder and then slowly started to walk towards a small copse of trees that lay a short distance from the road. As he got closer he saw the movement again. As he had hoped, it was one of the horses. Luan stopped and then bent down and pulled a bunch of dried grass. He walked forward slowly, holding the grass out in front of him and talking in a low voice. The words made no sense, "there you go, alright boy, go on then" but Luan knew it was the tone that made the

difference. Slowly he moved forward, then stopped as the horse made a tentative move towards him, and then slowly forward again and gradually the gap between the boy and the horse reduced.

Meanwhile, Bridie was keeping herself busy. After making sure that Mack was as comfortable as possible, she turned her attention to the slaver. The body lay crumpled on the road and Bridie was amazed that someone who had seemed so terrifying in life now seemed small and insignificant. Perhaps it had never been the person she was scared of, perhaps it was everything they signified. Bridie wasn't squeamish about bodies, and she quickly searched the corpse for anything useful. In fact it was only the smell that she found difficult; stale sweat and a musky odour that reminded her of captivity. There wasn't much to find but she took the cloak of black wool as a covering for Mack. There was also a rough belt carrying a pouch with a few coins and a small bone handled knife. It was far too big for her so she buckled it and pulled it over her head and arm so it lay crossways across her body. Then she walked back up the track looking for the place where Luan had first clashed with the rider. She soon spotted the object of her search gleaming faintly in the dirt. It was the bronze spearhead, still attached to about a forearm length of the wooden shaft. Bridie picked it up and hefted it in her hand, it would make a vicious weapon, easily concealed but deadly at close quarters, and a hard smile flitted round her face.
"Hey!" Bridie turned to see Luan, a big smile on his face,

leading a horse.
"I've found a horse!" He said, unnecessarily.
Bridie looked at the horse, which stared back nervously. It was a scrawny, unkempt beast, clearly not well looked after, with a bridle made from an old piece of rope and a tattered blanket for a saddle. But to Bridie it seemed that there was still some spirit there and she instantly took a liking to the animal.
"He's lovely!" she exclaimed. "What's his name?"
Luan was taken aback. "No idea. I just thought it would help with Mack, does it matter?"
"Of course it matters! Let's call him Dapple."
Luan was starting to feel that the conversation was getting away from him.
"You can't call him Dapple. He's brown."
"What difference does that make?"
"Dapple would be grey; you could call him Chestnut."
"I don't like the name Chestnut!" Bridie was now stroking the horse's head and mane and making cooing noises.
Luan decided to let it go.
"I thought we could use him to carry Mack, and also the horse..."
"Dapple!"
"...found a path..."
"Clever Dapple!"
"... going away from the road. It starts just beyond that copse of trees."

Getting Mack onto Dapple's back was so difficult that at

one point Luan thought they would never do it. Eventually he managed to get Mack's limp body over his shoulder and with Bridie pulling from one side and Luan pushing from the other they got him into place. They had to tie his feet to the stirrups and then his arms around the horse's neck to keep him on and Bridie had tears in her eyes by the time they were done. She covered him with the black cloak and then led the horse carefully off the road, talking softly all the time as they crossed the field. Luan wasn't sure he she was talking to reassure Mack, the horse, or herself. Perhaps it was all three.

To Luan the next three days blurred into each other. It started raining soon after they left the road and at first it was welcome, a grey curtain that hid them from the eyes of those that would follow, but any benefit was soon forgotten as their clothes became soaked and the ground underfoot turned to mud. They trudged onwards; following the path, no longer sure of the direction with no breaks in the thick blanket of cloud to consult sun or stars. No landmarks were visible beyond the veils of rain that reduced the muted landscape to the fields immediately around them. At night they huddled beneath what shelter they could find, trying to keep Mack warm, unable to light a fire. At some point on the second day Mack seemed closer to consciousness, he cried out and then began to talk but it was impossible to make out what he was saying and he showed no sign of hearing them when they spoke. He began to move as well, his arms would twitch or suddenly flail about before subsiding and once he sat up on the horse and gazed about him but before Bridie could respond he slumped back down into whatever private world he occupied. Throughout this time Bridie stayed close to him, leading Dapple carefully and trying at all times to keep the old man warm and comfortable.

It was late on the third afternoon when the path started to widen, eventually becoming a narrow lane with an earth bank on one side. On the other a rough hedge interspersed with trees offered some relief from the rain. The going got slightly easier and they made better time. Looking up to his left Luan saw that there was a narrow band of clear sky at the horizon, the weather was changing at last. Then the orange orb of the sun appeared below the cloud throwing its rays horizontally across the landscape. As the last of the rain died away an orange glow lit up the sides of trees and hedgerows and Luan felt a welcome warmth on his cheek as the light hit him. But all too soon it died away as the sun dipped below the hills, the last orange hues disappeared and the shadows lengthened into dusk.
"Look!" Bridie was pointing away to the south. A flickering light, then another appeared, and then more and more.
"Looks like someone lighting torches." Luan peered in their direction but he could make nothing out in the gathering gloom. They continued along the path until it abruptly ended at a wider track which seemed to head directly for the lights.

"Luan?" Bridie's tone was almost pleading, "Can't we try there? Mack needs help and we all need proper food and rest, even Dapple, I don't think we can go on like this!"
Luan didn't want to take the risk but he could hear the truth in Bridie's words. What was the use in trying to keep out of danger if they were frozen or starved? He nodded and they turned southwards.

It took them less than an hour. Rising before them was a wall made out of undressed wood, with a high gate. Torches lined the compound. Luan paused but then hammered on the gate, not knowing what to expect. This was no ordinary farm or small holding. Beyond the wall he could make out tall buildings rising in the darkness but these were unlit and hard to see in any detail. Bridie turned to him with an anxious look.
"Can you hear anything?"
"No," he replied but then his ears caught the sound of footsteps. "Wait, someone's coming."
A small flap opened in the gate and a pair of eyes peered through, flickering bright in reflected torchlight.
"Hmm. What have we here?" The voice was strong and clear with a hint of humour. Luan stepped forward.
"We are travellers. We were waylaid on the road and we have an injured man. Can you help us?"
"Please?" added Bridie in a plaintive voice. The eyes regarded them again.
"Hmm. A little one, a sick one, a four legged one. Harmless enough! But you, young man, have a sword! Dangerous

thing that, might hurt someone!"
Luan didn't know if the voice was serious or not. "I carry it to the guild house at Sanlynn. I mean you no harm, I give you my word!"
The voice laughed. "Your word eh? Easy to give it but then you've got to keep it as well! That's the hard part!"
Luan turned to Bridie who shrugged but then just as she was about to ask again they heard the sound of bolts being drawn and the gate opened inwards.
"Come on in then, don't hang about!"
They we're ushered in by a short, rather stout man almost entirely enveloped in a black robe. His short hair and beard were entirely white and his eyes glittered blue above chubby cheeks. Around his neck he wore a thick chain. He closed the gate behind them, bolting and locking it securely and then turned and folding his hands in a rather formal way he spoke.
"My name is Conn, the warden of the gate, and I welcome you to the House of Collection."

Twelve – The House of Collection

"You will learn to fight with sword and spear, weapons that you heft in your hand and feel their comforting weight. But remember, a true warrior uses whatever weapons he has at his disposal and not all of them take physical form. In the end knowledge may become the greatest weapon you possess. So I say to you these final words: Train hard, study tirelessly and learn well, that you may take your place among the ranks of the Klaideem."

Bridie felt nervous. Although she was sure that they could not have managed much longer on their own, and she was dreadfully worried about Mack, this was not what she had expected. She found the welcome strange and disturbing; and as they followed Conn she put her hand inside her jacket and touched the cold, hard metal of the spearhead for reassurance.

Conn led them along a passage way made up of rough-hewn logs which opened out into an open space with an earth floor, trodden hard with much use. Looking around she could see the line of torches that marked the wall curving round with various low structures set against it. The warden clapped his hands and two people dressed in brown robes appeared and ran towards them. Conn spoke some words in a tongue that Bridie did not recognise, and the two figures bobbed in agreement before starting to take Mack down from the horse.

"Wait! Where are they taking him?"
"He will be well looked after." Conn's tone was kind but firm. "You must come with me."
"We need to stay together." Luan stood with shoulders squared, his mouth set in a firm line.
"You have entered our world and you must abide by our rules." The words were not to be argued with but Conn smiled reassurance. "There is no enemy to fight here, leantor-cosan."
Luan paused. The salutation spoke to him in a way he did not understand. He looked at Bridie and she nodded briefly, confirming his instinct.
"Very well," he said, "we will go with you."
The two brown robed figures carried Mack to one of the low buildings at the edge of the compound. Bridie followed them and then returned a few minutes later to report that Mack was in bed and being cared for. Another of the brown robed figures came and took Dapple away to the stable and then Conn led the two young friends across the compound. Luan tried to work out how large the open area was but struggled in the darkness to make sense of it. He was starting to think that the whole place was built on a much bigger scale than he had first imagined. In front of him a sense of looming blackness started to coalesce into a solid cone like shape and he realised that the whole compound surrounded a flat topped hill. Directly in front of them two standing stones supported a rough lintel, the space between them an impenetrable velvet darkness.

Bridie felt a sudden pang of fear and without conscious thought she stepped closer to Luan and gripped his arm. Conn turned as if he sensed her disquiet.
"It looks worse than it is," he reassured her, and then he spoke to them both. "Search your hearts. Can you truly say that you mean us no harm?"
"None," replied Luan, again feeling the strange formality of the question.
"Of course not!" Bridie's tone was indignant. Conn smiled at her response and spoke again in that curiously formal way:
'Then have no fear and follow," and stepping between the stones, he disappeared. Luan hesitated only for a second and then followed, leaving Bridie alone on the threshold. In that moment the fear returned stronger than ever and try as she might she could not will her feet to move. ‘This is ridiculous!' she thought, furious with herself. 'I've lived with fear since I ran away from home,' but this was fear of the unknown. Tears started from her eyes as she stood there immobile. In the end it was simply the need not to be left alone that dragged her feet forward as she half threw herself through the doorway.

She stumbled forward, caught herself before she fell and then stopped in amazement. She had been expecting darkness but instead she was in a light and airy room with a high ceiling and walls of pale stone blocks jointed neatly together. In front of her a flight of wide steps led downwards and at the bottom stood Luan, his hand held out

to her.
"Come on," he said. "He's waiting"
Bridie glanced over her shoulder. Instead of the sheet of blackness the door way was filled with a veil of mist through which she could still make out the buildings in the courtyard from which they had come.
"Bridie?" Luan called her again and this time she made her way down the steps towards him.
"Where are we?" she asked as they met. Luan shrugged.
"I don't know," he said, "but it's like nowhere I've been before"
"Come!" Conn's voice called from further up the long corridor. They followed, and as they got to him he turned and led them into a large circular space.
"The Room of Discerning," he announced. Directly opposite them there was a doorway, clearly their intended exit, but the inhabitants of the room took all other thoughts from their minds. The room was home to a pack of wolves.

Bridie immediately sensed that something wasn't right. She was used to seeing wolves hunting in her clan's lands, in fact her clan respected them as agile and clever hunters, and they rarely bothered with humans. But these wolves were not behaving as she would expect, and they seemed larger and more aware, looking keenly at the newcomers, eyes bright with intelligence.
"What are they?" she asked. Luan looked at her sharply, surprised by her question. Unfamiliar with wolves, he had seen an obvious, if daunting, threat.

Conn smiled at her. "Clever girl! These are the discerning beasts. Wolves are ever sensitive to the moods and intentions of others, whether they are wolf kind or not. But these are something different. These are Wolf Clan, wolves that have grown up as part of a mixed human and wolf pack. They are exceptionally sensitive to humans. They can sense your feelings, gauge your intentions, and almost see into your soul. All who enter must walk through this room. The wolves will know if someone means us harm. If they come here with good intentions then no harm will come to them."
"And if they don't?" Luan could guess the answer to his question.
Conn shrugged. "Well, a wolf needs to eat!"
Looking across the open space, Luan hoped their guide was joking, but suspected that he wasn't. Even though Luan knew he carried no ill will, he still feared the test. What if the wolves mistook his fear and caution for animosity? Even if the wolves were perfectly safe it still took substantial courage to walk out into the midst of the pack. He breathed deeply and tried to build up his nerve.
"Come on then!" To Luan's amazement Bridie walked straight out into the middle of the room. His heart in his mouth, Luan watched as the largest wolf padded up to her. Bridie stopped, held her clenched fist over her heart, and bowed.
"Greetings revered pack leader," She said, without any sign of fear. The wolf took a step towards her and rested his muzzle lightly on her bowed head, then as Bridie

straightened up the wolf sat back on his haunches and thumped his tail twice, for all the world like a contented dog. It continued to sit there, tongue hanging out the side of its mouth as Bridie reached forward and stroked the top of its head.
"What's the matter Luan?" she said teasingly, "Scared?"
Luan sighed and started towards her, a startled Conn hurrying after.
"Is she always like this?" He asked.
"I'm afraid so." Luan replied.

After the Room of Discerning they followed a short corridor which opened onto a long hallway with doors at regular intervals.
"The guest quarters." Conn explained and he opened two adjacent doors. "I'm thinking that food and sleep is what you want most right now, although a wash wouldn't hurt either!" Luan was suddenly aware of the dirt of several days travelling and Bridie looked down at her clothes. Conn noticed and added "If you leave you clothes outside the door, they will be washed and returned to you."
The room was small and simply furnished but after days on the road a simple bed was luxury to Luan. On the small table stood a bowl and a chunk of bread. The stew was savoury and delicious but Luan was almost too hungry to notice. He stripped off his dirty clothes, left them outside the door, propped the sword in the corner of the room and then climbed under the warm covers and fell into a deep sleep.

Luan awoke with that delicious feeling that he had slept long and deeply. He got out of bed, washed and then dressed himself in the robe of coarse spun wool that he found at the foot of his bed. He almost expected his door to be locked but found it open and he called to Bridie and then knocked at her door. Trying the handle he found a room very similar to his but empty, there was no sign of her.
"Ah! Up at last are we?" Conn was making his way down the corridor. "Don't worry, she's fine. Up well before you, breakfasted and now she's with one of my brothers."
"Brothers?"
"In a sense." Conn paused. "Maybe it is time I explained what we do here. Come on!" He set off back down the corridor. Luan followed.

"We call this the House of Collection," Conn began, and what we collect is information."
"What sort of information?" Luan asked.
"Any sort and every sort." his guide replied. "You see the thing about information is that it is very hard to predict what you will need in the future. Things that seem important now will be insignificant in a couple of years' time. Something that went unnoticed years ago suddenly seems important now. So we collect everything."
Luan thought about this. "So who do you collect it for?"
Conn chuckled. "An exceedingly good question young man. Come let me show you something." He led Luan down a short flight of steps into a room that was like

nothing that Luan had ever seen before.

Luan's experience of art up to this point was almost non-existent. The embroidered blankets and woven rugs of his home had been decorative but nothing compared to the images that now confronted him. The room was a long narrow rectangle, lit by skylights. At the far end steps led up to a doorway identical to the one that Luan had entered by and along each side the walls were divided into a series of panels. Each panel held a painting of such skill that at first Luan thought he was looking a series of windows until he realised that each held a different view.
"The Room of Visions," Conn announced as he started walking the length of the room. Luan followed him, staring at the pictures, drinking in images of mountains, forests, lakes and seashores. Some of the landscapes seemed familiar, others strange and exotic. One portrait gave Luan a jolt of recognition, a man in a long grey cloak, face shrouded in a hood leaving only the eyes visible.
"The Walkers!"
Conn stopped and joined Luan in front of the picture.
"The Walker, in fact. He was the first one."
Luan was intrigued. "Who was he?"
"Nobody knows." Conn shrugged. "It is very frustrating. All we know is that he appeared during the wars of succession after the death of Amhar. It was a terrible time, the land was in ruins, crops burned, people starved. Then came the Walker, preaching that the land had to be healed and that the only way was to walk the paths. He attracted

followers and they still walk the paths to this day."
"I met some of them." Luan paused. "It was strange, for a moment I wanted to join with them."
"I have talked with those who have walked the paths," replied Conn. "It is a strange compulsion. Some are in its grip for their entire lives, others for a shorter time, perhaps only a few years. Those who have fallen under its spell cannot explain it, but say that their lives are richer. They feel a deep contentment."
He gazed again on the painting before walking on along the room.

A few moments later Luan stopped before one of the paintings that he felt he should recognise, a seascape with five tall ships sailing towards a setting sun. The ships were wreathed in must which blurred the distinction between sea and sky, and the whole painting glowed with the diffused light of the sunset. The still water was a sheet of living gold.
"The first voyage of Amhar." Conn spoke at Luan's side.
"It's like a dream I had," the young man replied. "I had forgotten, but now it feels so real, like if I closed my eyes I could step into it."
Conn gave Luan a worried glance "Please don't!" he said. Luan wasn't sure if he was joking.
"Is this the collection?" He asked.
"It is a tiny fraction," Conn replied. "These are the ones that seem to have the most significance, although we don't always understand why that is, and it isn't just paintings.

Let me show you." He led the way out of the Room of Visions, and down a long corridor from which opened a series of small rooms. Seemingly at random Conn stopped and gestured for Luan to enter. Luan stepped into a space that was really only big enough for one, like a walk in cupboard, with shelves full of books and scrolls from floor to ceiling on each wall. Luan was staggered.

"If each of the rooms is as full as this one, then the must be..."
"Thousands of books?" Conn finished the sentence for him, "indeed there are! Stories, poems, sketches, dramas, history, and books on any subject you can imagine. And that's not all, come on!" The last words were spoken over his shoulder as Conn set off down the corridor. Luan took a last look round the shelves and then hurried after.

Up yet another flight of steps the corridor opened out into a much grander space. The long hall was brightly lit with floor to ceiling windows at intervals on both sides and the walls and ceiling shone with decoration.
"The Hall of Maps," announced Conn.
As they walked along Luan realised that the tapestries that lined the walls were actually detailed maps, finely woven and illustrated with pictures. Each panel on the ceiling also contained a beautifully painted map. Luan had thought himself quite familiar with maps. His father had one of the family lands detailing the farms and small holdings throughout. Marius had sometimes brought maps when he

visited and Luan had always been fascinated, stealing a glimpse when he could and carrying away images of roads and mountains in faraway places with strange sounding names. He had the same feeling now, only one of the maps seemed familiar, that showing the kingdom, the rest were of countries he didn't recognise. As Conn led him further down the hall Luan began to grasp the enormity of what was happening. The House of Collection was a treasure trove of knowledge, so much information all gathered together in one place it didn't seem possible.
"I expect you're wondering how we do it." Conn seemed to read the boy's mind. "I'll show you."
They had reached the end of the hall and a spiral staircase led them down into a large open area with doors regularly spaced along the walls. Some of the doors were open and the rooms beyond looked empty, Luan caught a glimpse of seating around a low stage, but some of the doors were closed and on each hung a sign with a symbol on it. There were quite a few people in the room, men and women all robed like Conn except that the belts of their robes were a variety of colours. They stood around talking quietly in small groups or sat on the benches that lined the walls. Each carried a small bag or bundle of papers. As Conn and Luan entered a tall man with a closely cut dark hair broke off his conversation and lifted his hand in welcome, his companion, a diminutive grey haired lady, looked at Luan with curiosity.

At that moment one of the closed doors opened and a group

of men and women came out, followed by an elderly man in a grey robe who lifted the sign down from the door and replaced it with another showing a different design. Immediately the groups around the room broke up in a sudden babble of noise as people made their way towards the room.
"Come on," said Conn and he led Luan across and into the room just as the grey robed man pulled the door shut. Conn sat down on one of the benches at the back of the room and pulled Luan down after him. There was seating for about twenty five people, although there were only about ten in the audience. Against the wall opposite the door was a low stage, on which sat an old man drinking a cup of water. On the wall behind him hung a row of symbols, the last of which was the same as that on the outside of the door. He put his cup down and looked up as one of the listeners asked him a question in a language that Luan did not recognise. The old man nodded and then started to talk in the same language. Luan looked round and saw that the audience were all making notes of some sort.
"What language is that?" Asked Luan, keeping his voice to a whisper. Even then he earned a disapproving glance from the grey robed man.
"Old Pirean," replied Conn, seemingly unconcerned.
"Pirean as in the Pireacht Empire?" The surprise showed in Luan voice. This time one of the listeners turned round and gave the pair a very pointed glance. Luan coloured in shame as Conn held up a pacifying hand and then without saying anything else he stood and led Luan out of the room.

The grey robed man let them out, clearly disapproving of their exit, but unable to speak without committing the same crime.

They sat on one of the benches outside while Conn explained to Luan what he had observed.
"The symbols are our code that allows everything to checked and cross referenced. No point in recording things if we can't find them when we need to!"
"I noticed that the symbol on the door matched one of the ones behind the speaker"
"Well spotted. That symbol tells the collectors, the observers as it were, the general area to be discussed, so those with a special interest know when to go in."
"So that's why there was a changeover." Luan was starting to understand.
"Exactly," replied Conn, "now imagine that going on all the time with many different people talking and answering questions and you start to see the enormity of our task."
"It's incredible," Luan agreed. "How do you choose the people to talk to you?"
"Well mostly we don't" replied Conn with a smile "Mostly they choose us!"
"You mean, like me and Bridie?"
"Yes. You see people tend to find us when they need help, and people who need help often have a story to tell. We help them and look after them and afterwards we ask them if they will tell us their stories. They nearly always do."
Luan thought about this. "So I will need to tell my story?"

"If you want."
"What if I make it up?"
Conn smiled again "We've been doing this for hundreds of years, so were getting quite good at knowing when someone is not telling the truth. Besides sometimes the stories people make up tell us more about them than the truth!"
Luan thought about this and decided it made some sort of sense.
"What about Mack?"
"Mack will be well looked after, and then when he is well enough he can decide if he wants to tell us his story."
"I'm sure Mack will talk to you," Luan replied. "Getting him to stop will be the hard part!"
Conn laughed at that and then Luan remembered something he had meant to ask.
"You said the man was speaking Old Pirean, what did you mean?"
"A good question," replied Conn, "and one that is best answered over food."
Luan suddenly realised how hungry he was, and readily agreed.

Conn led them through a maze of corridors and finally into a large refectory, lit by high windows of coloured glass along each side which threw patches of colour across the floor. At one end of the room people queued at several serving hatches before taking their food and sitting down at one of the three benches that ran the length of the room.

They joined one of the queues and were each soon served a tray which they took back to a table. Luan looked at his food with interest: there was some dark bread with butter, a bowl of porridge and a thick slice of cheese, as well as a beaker holding a sweet smelling drink. He nodded in approval, not a bad breakfast. For a few minutes both he and Conn focused on the business in hand, but then Conn pushed his empty bowl aside, took a sip of his drink and then began.
"The lands that we call the Pireacht Empire have been in existence for a long time, longer than the kingdom that you call home. Over such a period of time history and legend blend together so that it difficult to know how much is real and how much is the imagination of minstrels and story tellers. What we do know though is that the starting point was a small mountainous country called Pirea, far to the south of the lands you have travelled. How that small country became a mighty empire is a mystery, but one that the man we heard this morning might just help us to unravel."
"Luan!" At that point they were interrupted by a small figure that landed with a bump on the bench next to Luan.
"Bridie...mmf!" the hug that squeezed the breath out of Luan cut him off short and prevented further speaking. Luan was dimly aware of a man behind him greeting Conn and indicating that he would collect some food. After a moment Bridie's grip slackened and Luan managed to disentangle himself.
"Oh Luan, this is so wonderful! Where have you been? I've

seen so many things! Have you seen the pictures? And all those books! Are you going to talk to them? Of course you are! I think I will..."
"Hello Bridie." Luan tried, unsuccessfully, to interrupt the flow. He smiled, conscious of how glad he was to see her as her chatter flowed on and on. He realised that he had rarely seen Bridie other than weighed down by anxiety, and he marvelled at the change in her.
"Are you listening to me at all?" She was looking at him with a hint of irritation.
"Of course," he said, and then decided it was good time to change the subject. "Have you seen Mack?"
"No" Bridie looked momentarily worried, and then perked up "But Drin, that's him over there getting the food, he's been ever so nice, has sent for word and we should know something soon he said."
"I too have asked for word to be sent," Conn added. "Mack will certainly be well cared for. In the meantime, eat!" and he gestured at Luan's tray.

Luan would always struggle to remember the next few days. Sessions spent telling his story, although interspersed with meals and sleeping, seemed to run together. He saw Bridie briefly at odd times when their paths crossed. The news that Mack had regained consciousness reassured them both but they were kept too busy and had no opportunity to visit him. Then one morning Luan awoke to find that he had no appointments to speak that day, it was like waking from a dream. He sat up in bed and looked at his sword that stood in the corner of his room, untouched since he had arrived. There was a part of him that dreaded picking it up, but he knew that the time had come. He got up, dressed, and then pulled the sword belt over his shoulder. He felt the weight as the sword settled into its familiar place and knew that he was making the right decision. It was time to be back on the sword path.

"I thought this might be the case." Conn stood in the open doorway, Bridie just behind him.

"Are you leaving?" she asked. Luan looked at her and saw that the smile of recent days had suddenly gone.

"It is time." He answered simply. Bridie turned away.

"I'll get my things." Her voice was quiet and subdued.

"No need." Luan called after her. She turned back towards him, her eyes suddenly wet with tears.

"What's do you mean?"

"I'm going on my own."

"But..."

"No, just listen. You need to stay here. You have much more to tell the collectors and someone needs to be here for Mack. Besides, when I get to Sanlynn I will go into the guild house, and you would be left alone and what would happen to you then?"

"I'd survive!" She said fiercely.

"I know you would." He smiled at her response. "But you need to stay." He paused and then added "Mack needs you more than I do." She hesitated for a moment and then suddenly dashed into the room and threw her arms around him, burying her face in his chest as she sobbed. For a moment Luan stood there, unsure, before slowly putting his arms around her. Sadness and an aching sense of loss welled up within him. Surprised by feelings he hadn't realised were there Luan realised that this parting was in some ways harder than leaving home. That had been anticipated and prepared for, balanced by the excitement and freedom of setting out on an adventure. This time he was leaving friends that he was bound to by ties forged in the challenge and danger of the road, friendship unlooked for but real and strong nonetheless.

After a visit to the refectory where they collected supplies for the journey, Conn led Luan up several flights of stairs, a way he hadn't been before. The stairs emerged in the centre of an octagonal room. Each the walls contained a doorway like the one through they had entered the House of Collection, sheets of mist with hints of a different view beyond.
"The house does not exist in the same world that you travel, as I am sure you realise," explained Conn, "which is why it is possible for each of these doorways to lead out into a different place." He indicated one of the doorways. "This one will actually put you within a day's march of Sanlynn"
"Thank you," said Luan and he walked up to the doorway.
"No thanks necessary," replied Conn, "it has been a pleasure to meet you. I'm glad it was my turn to serve as warden on the day you arrived. Now go, young leantor-cosan, I wish you safe travel and successful studies. It may well be that if the fates smile upon you and you are

successful that we may meet again. Until then farewell!"
"Farewell!" echoed Luan and he stepped through the doorway.

There was a moment of dizziness and then Luan was standing on a hilltop, the breeze blowing in his hair. Around him were the stones and turf covered mounds of a ruin. Behind him a passageway led into the hill. Before him the land spread out in a patchwork of fields. In the distance faint pillars of smoke betrayed the presence of a large town. It was a fine morning. For a moment he missed Bridie and Mack but although he was alone, he didn't feel lonely. "After all, I started out on my own," thought Luan, "and now I shall finish on my own." There was a pleasing symmetry to it. Luan smiled and set off down the hill.

I hope you liked *The Path of Swords*, this first episode in Luan's adventure. Obviously we can't leave him there, and his story continues in *The Guild of Warriors*, due for release in October 2017. Keep reading for a sneak preview!

But first I would appreciate it if you would consider leaving a review. It would mean a lot to me and doesn't have to be too long or time consuming.

Also you might like to know more about my writing. You can get a free story and sign up for updates etc. here:

http://eepurl.com/cEVFcL

You can also visit my blog at:

www.someidiottalking.wordpress.com

I'd love to hear from you.

Now read on for *The Guild of Warriors* Chapter One.

There are four physical pre-requisites to being a swordsman: Strength, speed, flexibility and fitness. It follows that a disciplined training program is the foundation upon which the way of the sword is built.

In any group of teenage boys there is always one who looks far too old to be there. Drustan was big, he was impressively muscled and had an extraordinary amount of facial hair for a thirteen year old. He wasn't stupid as such, it was just that he had never really had to think about anything very hard and so he tended not to bother. Right now he was complaining.

"I don't see why we have to do this unarmed nonsense, I mean, I'm going to be a swordsman, a warrior. I'm not going to turn up to battle without a weapon am I? So what's the point? Aaaaaaaagghhhhhh!"

Drustan's final comment occurred as he gracefully sailed into the air, propelled by a diminutive woman who had walked quietly into the room while he was talking.

She rolled to her bare feet as Drustan hit the floor with a solid thump.
"I am Sargent Crow and that little demonstration shows you that fighting is not all about size or strength."
She wore a soft leather tunic and leggings and her black

hair was tied back and plaited. She may have been small but stood hands on hips as if she owned the room. Above her welcoming smile her eyes were hard.

Behind her Drustan climbed to his feet and looked round angrily for his attacker.

“The combination of surprise, agility and the techniques I teach will give you the advantage in any combat situation,” Sargent Crow continued.

Behind her Drustan clasped his hands together and raised them like a club above the slight woman's head.

“Although...” Crow suddenly spun on the spot, her left foot lashing out to land solidly between Drustan’s legs. “...a good hard kick in the privates is also extremely effective!”

With a noise that sounded a bit like “Arfuzle” Drustan turned cross-eyed and sank slowly to the floor. A few grins flashed around. Drustan wasn't the most popular boy in the group and some of the smaller boys cheered up noticeably.

Luan had been at the guild for just over two weeks. He had reached the outskirts of Sanlynn after a day’s hard walking, just as a fine mist of rain brought on an early dusk.

Originally a walled town, the growing city had overflowed its confines and spilled out along the roads. Some of the houses outside the walls were sturdy and well built, but many were little more than wretched hovels. Rubbish and effluent filled the ditches at the side of the road and the smell at times was almost overpowering. Dogs rooted in the rubbish, snapping and growling as they contested the few edible morsels. Soon the street became lined with inns and shops giving the area a more prosperous feel but Luan could see that down the narrow side alleys the slums were never far away. Many of the shops were closing, a few of the proprietors called out to him as he passed but most concentrated on taking in their wares and pulling down the shutters. By contrast the inns seemed to be readying themselves for business and from one the sound of a fiddle being tuned reminded Luan of Mack and he smiled to himself. A girl called out from an open window, inviting him in. She looked young but her eyes betrayed a different story. His glance took in her lank hair and a dress that had seen better days; he blushed, mumbled a polite refusal and walked on. Her laugh followed him down the street like a malignant wasp.

The wall of the old town had once been imposing but now it seemed to sag like the belly of the solitary guard at the gate. Torches guttered above the rusted portcullis and reflected off the puddles below. The rain had thickened and

the guard was clearly reluctant to leave what little shelter he had. Eyes squinting from under the brim of his over large helmet, he decided that Luan posed little threat, and waved him through. The street was not as wide but better made and the houses larger and well-constructed. Solid oak timbers, glass windows and here and there even some old stone work showed that the wall was clearly a social barrier if no longer a defensive one. After about ten minutes' walk the street opened onto a large square. On three sides it was bordered by large houses, on the fourth by the tall wall of the guild-house of the Klaideem. In a stark contrast to the town gate, the guards here were alert and business like, uniforms smart and weapons sharp.
"State your business." The flat stare of the guard did nothing to calm Luan's nerves.
"I've come to join," he said without thinking. The first guard managed to keep a straight face, but the second snorted convulsively as he tried to stifle a laugh.
"Join?" the first guard replied. "What do you think this is? Play time?"
Luan was stung by the words but before he could reply the second guard came to his defence.
"Leave the boy be Hwl." He smiled at Luan. "Come on lad, try again."
Luan drew himself up and paused and then answered.
"My name is Luan, second son of Garioch, Cunbran of the house of Artran and I follow the path of swords!"

"Hail sword brother, may you bring honour to this your house," the guard called Hwl replied and this time he smiled warmly. "Well said lad!" added his companion. "Come on, I'll take you to the Captean."
He led Luan through the gate and into a small room that opened off the main passage. Behind a desk an older man sat, writing by the light of a lantern.
"New recruit Captean," called out the guard.
The man behind the desk looked up. He had a hard face, weathered and brown with lines deeply etched. On the left a vicious scar ran from jaw to hairline, covered in part by a black eye patch. It continued as a white streak into hair that was black and wiry with a touch of grey around the temples. The Captean's single eye glittered as his gaze swept over Luan. When he spoke his voice was unexpectedly soft.
"Your name boy?"
This time Luan was determined to get it right.
"Luan ap Garioch, second son of the house of Artran."
The Captean pulled a large book towards him, opened it and started to write. "Welcome to the Guildhouse," he said. "In a moment Cail here will show you to your quarters but first I must ask something of you." He held out his hands, palms up. "Your sword if you will."
Reluctantly Luan undid the buckle and held it out. The Captean took it, weighed it in his hands and then pulled the blade a short way from the scabbard.

"This is a fine weapon! Where do you get it?"
"It was my uncle's," Luan replied.
"I recognise this blade." The Captean's gaze examined Luan again. "And now I recognise you. You're Marius' nephew aren't you?"
"You knew him?" Luan suddenly felt a hunger to know more about his uncle.
"Knew him? I fought alongside him! He was a true Klaideem, and a good friend." He paused, lost for a moment in memory, and then shook his head. "A sad loss".
The Captean stood and walked over to a bench. He picked up a rag and a small jar. "A sword such as this needs to be well looked after," he said, drawing the blade. He uncorked the jar, held the rag to it and upended it twice in quick succession. Then holding the rag folded double between the thumb and forefinger of his left hand, he pulled the sword slowly through.
"A trace of blood here I think?" He said holding out the stained rag. "You've used this sword in anger haven't you boy?"
Luan nodded. "I had to."
"Who was he?"
"A slaver." Luan felt he should explain. "He was going to hurt my friends."
"Dead?"
"Yes." Luan still felt a tug of guilt.
"Good!" The Captean nodded in satisfaction. "Don't you

worry about that scum." He held the sword up, twisted his wrist so he could see both sides and, satisfied, slid it back into the scabbard. He looked up at Luan. "Do you want to know the secret of being a great warrior, boy?"
"Yes please," replied Luan.
"Not dying!" The Captean snorted a laugh. "You survived your first fight, and you made it here. That's two victories Luan, make sure you count them all."
"I will." Luan noticed that the Captean no longer called him 'boy'.
"Cail will show you to your quarters," the Captean was all business now, "but I am afraid the sword stays here."
Luan felt like he had been punched "No!" He almost shouted. The Captean looked at him.
"Think about it Luan. We can't have young boys running round with swords. Someone would get hurt. No. The blade stays here; it will lie in the Chapel of Swords until you reclaim it."
"When will that be?" asked Luan.
"When you are a Klaideem," the Captean replied.

Printed in Poland
by Amazon Fulfillment
Poland Sp. z o.o., Wrocław